DATE DUE

DEC 1 7 2014			

D1160895

KENNETH KOCH

HOTEL LAMBOSA

AND OTHER STORIES

COFFEE HOUSE PRESS :: MINNEAPOLIS :: 1993

Many stories in this book have previously appeared in the following periodicals: *Boulevard, American Poetry Review, Raritan, The Paris Review, Scripsi, The World, Erato, Kenyan Review,* and *New American Writing*.

For editorial assistantce with these stories I am much indebted to Jordan Davis; for some of the inspiration to write them to the Palm-o-the-Hand Stories of Yasunari Kawabata.

The publishers would like to thank the following funders for assistance which helped make this book possible: the Bush Foundation; the Minnesota State Arts Board; the Andrew W. Mellon Foundation; and the Lila Wallace Reader's Digest Fund.

Coffee House Press books are available to the trade through our primary distributor, Consortium Book Sales & Distribution, 1045 Westgate Drive, Saint Paul, MN 55114. For personal orders, catalogs, or other information, write to:
Coffee House Press
27 North Fourth Street, Suite 400
Minneapolis, MN 55401

Library of Congress Cataloging in Publication Data
Koch, Kenneth, 1925-
    Hotel Lambosa, and other stories / by Kenneth Koch.
       p. cm.
    ISBN 1-56689-008-x : $10.95
    I. Title.
    PS3521.027H6 1993
    813'.54—dc20   93-17101, CIP

CONTENTS

To Karen

ANTONELLOS

Janice and I decided to look for every Antonello da Messina in Sicily. Mostly portraits, they had a noble clarity and the suggestion of a quick intimacy that was obviously more than one could hope for with persons so grand. There weren't very many of them and Sicily wasn't very large; but there were twenty of them and Sicily, if you subdivide its size by its means of transportation, is five times as big as the United States. We were looking at inaccessibility, and no doubt about it. There was one supposed Antonello hung in a chapel on the side of a cliff, I couldn't imagine how anyone but a goat would manage to get there. Four of the paintings were in cities that were easy to reach. The rest were really, it seemed, randomly scattered all over that savage island, which was not exactly organized to assist one in the task of seeing them.

We had to content ourselves with seeing six, which wasn't bad, given our limited means, of money, transportation, and time. My father was propositioned by a young Sicilian man, who offered him sex in exchange for money, but my father refused. My mother encouraged the local "artists-for-tourists" by purchasing samples of their work. Janice's and my daughter, Melissa, was only a tiny girl then (two years old) and she was featured in many, many photographs, most of them shot on the elegant grounds of a large hotel built into or inspired by a monastery—I forget its name. What do you think about this situation, Stuart? my mother said. What situation? said my father. The fact that Kenny and Janice pay so little attention to us? Melissa! Melissa! she called the tiny girl. Come back from the edge of that garden. She might fall off. My father went and picked up Melissa. He was wearing a white suit and smoking a Lucky Strike. At home he had a Buick but here he had a rented Peugeot. I don't know why he didn't have a Fiat but he had a Peugeot. Stuart! What, Lillian? My father was holding Melissa now by the hand and he was smiling as she was attempting to lead him around. This way! This way, Dumpa! she said. Well, you haven't answered my question, said my mother. Well, Lillian. My father smoked. At this moment Janice and I appeared around the hotel bend. We found a new Antonello, I said. And some peaches, cried Janice. Here, look! I've never tasted anything so delicious in my life, said my mother. Janice picked up Melissa and gave her a big kiss. Hello, Baby! Mamam mama, Melissa said, agitating and pointing. There was something she wanted Janice to see. Two rabbits were holding completely still in the garden. A blue-and-red-feathered bird—what was it? it couldn't be a parrot—landed near them and still they didn't move. Oh, how wonderful! Janice said. Then she hesitated, and my mother changed her facial expression. We shouldn't go any closer or they'll be frightened. How was your morning, Lillian, Janice said, holding tight to one hand of Melissa and approaching my mother's chair. At this, my mother got up, raising herself as if it were difficult and saying something like "Oooohf!" You don't know what it's like to get old, she said.

Janice and I looked beyond the family's doings to the exquisite tone, pathos, dramatic poses, and coloring of Antonello's paintings. As often as not, we were walking about with some form of the following sentence in our heads: "Antonello introduced easel painting into Italy." He found it in Holland. That meant that, before him, everything that was painted in Italy had been frescoes or paintings on wood. Antonello ruined painting—frescoes were better! Antonello saved painting! Where could it have gone, that wall-dependent art? These ideas were nourishment to us. A wide-brimmed hat above her and with my father standing at her side, my mother in the hotel garden breathed the Sicilian air.

WIND

The wind was blowing very hard. Don't, she said. I can't stand here. Someone will pinch my derrière. Well all right let's keep walking, the young man said. They were standing in front of an art gallery in Florence. The works inside it were hysterically bad. They were comprised of button shapes of all colors arranged as if the canvasses were coats. There were twenty-four of them. At the back of the gallery in a smaller room there was a smaller show of someone who painted apparently only squiggles. On a white background you'd find squiggles of gold, green, and navy blue. Usually it was just one color to each work. The two walked along but they had little more to say to each other. He had shown her his interest in the physical side of her, and she had shown him her toughness and her know-how and her at this moment not wanting what he wants. So they are even. Each has shown an attractive quality, desire and refusal, and there is not much more for them to do. In six or seven years perhaps or maybe eight, some equally windy day, she herself will have her paintings in a gallery, and she will say, when some man says the way she looks, the way she is, drives him crazy, she will say, Does it, do I really? Well, it's nice to know one is pleasing. Have you seen the work? When the young man who turns out to be the same one says yes that he has and he likes it but that he doesn't wish to talk about that, she says Oh! and he then Do you remember me, from seven or eight years ago in Florence? It was an example of bad behavior on my part, liking you, but I did nonetheless—I don't know. She said, What are you saying?

4

EM PORTUGUÊS

They were listening to the fados, sung one after another. Each fado sang of the scorched terrible unsatisfiable lost wretchedness of love. There is no happy side, except for intensity of feeling, to a fado song. They felt the excessively narrow reality of the fados shoving into and bumping them, like a drunk. The man's hand untightened itself from the woman's after the momentous finale of the song. As they got up to go back to the Hotel of Ionia and of Camoëns, they were accosted by a waiter at the exit, saying You forgot your coats. We didn't wear any coats. My love is gone, my heart is like a smashed mask of glass. If my shoeprints are steeped in your blood, woman, you will know that I have come back. Those coats belong to somebody else.

THE VILLINO

My wife and I were waiting for the train to come that would take us from Rome to Florence. She had on a bright pink dress and a white straw hat with a yellow bow around it. I was wearing some old khaki army trousers and a dark green canvassy sort of shirt. I didn't wear a hat, so, as soon as any evidence of the train came by, I could see it. It was some leaves, swirling in an arc lamp over our heads. Look, Janice, I said. The train is coming. And she said Oh then looked down the tracks the train came and we got on it.

The train stopped at Viterbo, Orvieto, Chianciano Terme, and Siena. It wasn't an express, that is, not what in Italy is called a Rapido, so it gave us a lot of time to enjoy the trip. The ride was bumpy and sometimes, even in between towns, the train would stop and we'd spend five minutes just waiting. At the stations I always looked around for a man or woman with a cart with drinks and things to eat on it but I never saw one.

Between Siena and Florence, my wife said, Well, what are we going to do when we get to Florence? I said, Find a pensione, first a place for tonight, then after a few days we can start to look for a regular place to stay. I'd like to do that as soon as we get there, she said. Oh no, not tonight, you know, but tomorrow if that's all right with you.

Well, it might be nice to look at a few things in the city, I said. More practically, I said, it might be good to get a sense of the city before we decide where we want to settle down. Yes, I guess that's right, Janice said, although I think her heart was more in getting settled as soon as we could.

Actually, by the end of the first day, it seemed to me amusing to start looking for a place. It was a change from regular touring to go into an office where there was a man in a coat tie and shirt who acted interested in helping us do something we wanted. Ah, I think I have just the thing, one such man said. But this was on the fourth day.

This man invited us into his car and drove us out to inspect the villino, where he proposed that we might like to live. He said, Here you may be very happy. And it is an advantageous price. We rented that house.

Now, thirty years later, I think I can still see that house very clearly. I can see the kitchen window through which she or I would sometimes (just idly) stare, because it was mostly from right there that we seemed nearest to the Italian song-singing by the housemaid next door. I most emphatically recall the gate, though what was its color— green? white?—where an "old man" (he may have been sixty, sixty-five, or seventy, but he was bent over) came, saying, when I walked down to open it, I am Ottavino, the peasant.

Janice's room and mine had in its center a fairly big bed. I wrote over here against this wall. In the living room of this villino there's a fireplace and it's truly needed, expensive as the wood may be, because the Italians think in Italy it never gets cold.

In this house some extraordinary things took place. One night we were leaving the house to go to the Florence Opera, to hear *Un Ballo in Màschera*, with Gianni Poggi. Janice adored and was fascinated by and was also somewhat amused by this tenor, Gianni Poggi. He had a beautiful lyrical tenor voice, and he sang in the new bel canto style with considerable sweetness and gusto. He was also short and plump. The skill and sweetness of this fat young man's singing was a reminder of the consuming and infinitely soothing unreality of art. Whenever, wherever we traveled, we seemed to run into operatic performances with Gianni Poggi. Who's singing tonight? I asked Janice. Who do you think? she said. Gianni Poggi! I remember a little moonlight circling her head, as she said that, and as we walked out, into that tender night, where later Gianni Poggi, all pudgy five feet of him, would sing, to a slightly taller soprano, "M'ami? m'ami? m'ami?" in such a way that it turned our hearts to stone, if stones could feel, could retain that warm night and that moonlight in their mass, and be as heavy ("M'ami?") as they are and as light as we were, when, without nervous impulses or headaches we would head back "home"—to the villino, which not three weeks before had been hung out on the road past the Ortopèdico a little sadly and emptily "for rent."

We probably paid about a hundred dollars more a month for that place than we should have. An agent told us this, the friend of a friend. John Fardras was renting some rooms in the Palazzo Gambolini and once on an exquisite warm and airy late spring evening, we broke our general pattern of behavior (mostly, if there was no opera, we stayed home) and went to his place. These rooms were very beautiful, at this old palace, and I thought it would have been a different destiny for us, maybe, if we had lived there. But there was no avoiding our house.

8

VENICE

I dreamed last night that Marcello told me it was too complicated. I had this dream last night. I wrote the libretto this past summer, in July.

Everything is a dream, said his friend. What's the difference if Marcello sets the libretto or not?

None, he said. But *you* write a libretto and then let's just see if you'd prefer to have it set or not. I'd like Marcello to set it, and Ronconi to direct it, and for there to be simultaneous performances outdoors above the Canal in Venice and at the Metropolitan Opera. That's what I want.

When I heard my wife's voice on the telephone, calling me in Venice from New York City, I knew that someone must have died. We didn't phone each other now about ordinary things.

Venice. The cemetery. Walking around. Arm in arm, sometimes. Occasionally, hand in hand. Her eyes look up. His eyes look down. They look down together. A grave.

Evening. Later. The shine of plates. The smile of knives and of forks.

Hotel. Stone balcony. Opposite church. Great big faces. Almost in the room. Stone they stare at them with their own face. And yet since it is Carnival he and she put on masks. One red mask his. One black mask hers. This is happiness. There is no other. Cold water faucet. A slight pain in the chest.

She takes. Opposite church. To miss what massive. Increasing silence. Man at the desk. Woman at the desk.

9

Dream band. Marchers off the street. Canal-side restaurant. No more eels! Isthmuses of islands.

I have. I have a reason. I have a reason to be sad. Here
is a reason to be joyful. A grass turf. A striped day. But,
most of all, this girl.

It became what it began to be: a cemetery. An island
dedicated to the dead.

Black were the gondolas in the canals, and black the
clothing that the gondoliers wore. Black were the but-
tons on the coat that he did not put on, to go out, because
it was spring. Black were the steps on the stairway when
he first came to them, blinded by the sun. And then his
body went off.

Again said Marcello, I said I won't set it and I won't.
It's too complicated. A librettist in writing should seek
only to inspire the writing of music. You haven't done
that.

I have more friends than you, Marcello, I said.

Ah, but they don't set libretti, Marcello said. But if I
don't set it, of course you are free to give it to someone
else. But here. Let me look at it one last time.

At this point I woke up. The complicated dream was
at an end. Actually, Morton had died, and I was walking
around thinking, thinking, whether I wanted to or not.
Thinking neither of Morton nor of the opera but of you.

NEGATIVE BLOOD

The car was long and blue, an Italian car, rather surprising that the young doctor should have such a nice one. But why shouldn't the young doctor have a blue car? It was an Alfa nineteen fifty-four. In the car there were two young persons as it drove across the Arno—a doctor and a young man, about thirty. They were driving to a Catholic hospital on the side of Florence toward Fiesole. On a stretcher on a bed in the civic hospital in Florence was the young man's wife, who needed the blood. There was said to be some in the hospital on the other side of the Arno. The baby had miscarried and was born dead in a violent hemorrhage. It wasn't, as they thought, placenta previa. They didn't know what it was. She was losing a lot of blood and needed more and there was a shortage of it. The nun walked up and past them, swinging her censer, and against her blue slightly bloused-out uniform he could see the big batch of keys that would be needed to get them into the room where the blood was stored. Forgive me, the doctor said. It's all right, the sister said. She interrupted the little service to save the young woman's life. It was a lucky chance that a container of A-RH-negative blood was there and had not been sent to Hungary along with all the other containers of blood for people in the failed rebellion against the Russians. It was nineteen fifty-six. His wife lived for twenty-five more years. For her, the experience of this night, while she was experiencing it, had nothing to do with driving, with nuns, with Hungary, but with one wild wish, that the baby not be dead, that she be herself again, and that she and the baby be together, as they had never been, but as she had imagined, for so many months now, that they would be.

AN ORACLE

Evan said, Don't ask me. About love. I'm not the one to know. Evan had flying folds of love like pennants and flags forever flying from his person. On the Greek island of Hydra girls flooded toward the piers in a parade, all of them loving Evan, begging him not to go away but happy to be begging, happy to be in Evanid procession, glad to be living in that moment, in Greece, in a twentieth-century peaceful day. This is one of your lobotomy perkings, said Evan. It isn't a "story," but it's not the truth. In a story was the development of character. Minna was very shy, bony, awkward. As her body grew to fullness, self-confidence came, and behold, she was a changed character. God, it's boring! Evan said. He looked at two rabbits who were holding stock-still after darting around. I'll tell you what you should do if you want to write a story. Just write down what you told me about Ellen. How you tried to find her. And then did. It makes a perfect story just that way. I suppose so, Herndon said. But he wasn't going to write it. He was dying to question Evan about love. No, said Evan. Yes. Listen. I am leaving this island. Never in my whole life will I come back to this island. I just know it, don't ask me why, I feel it in my bones. My *bones,* he emphasized, grinning and gritting his jaws. My bee-hee-ho-ho-ho-ho-hones. My bonezeezee. What is love, Evan? Stay away from women, Evan said. And certainly from men. Then at least you'll have some chance of finding out. Good-bye. They went on suspecting, as Evan got into the boat, and away, that like everybody else, he knew more about it than he had told.

Don't expect anything, said Evan. And, You'll get the

payback soon. Be *careful*. Just forget it. Get over. He was a major general in the wars of love. I'm just kidding but seriously, he said. Get out of it what you can. He went into the toilet. It was hard to hear him through the door. I was afraid I'd missed something. I said, What did you say? Nothing! said Evan. It doesn't matter what you say or what anybody says. But probably the less you say the better off you'll be. They remember *everything*. He likes the harem effect, he said about one. Oh, they're absolutely wonderful, Evan said. Don't get me wrong. He said, Good. Enjoy it. You know, there's not so much time. Hello, Angel, Evan said. The true history of Evan can never be told—because he is always telling it himself, as advice and proverbs. He knows it, too. I have become my admirers, said Evan, quoting Auden (about Yeats). Or rather, not exactly—s-zzz-miling: I have become my *con*fer*ees!*

What else did Evan know? With determination one can get to the bottom of a thing. He wanted to be close but not too close.

After each encounter he wanted still to be completely himself. I don't blame him.

Still, what would be wrong with being slightly influenced? No one has ever seen him slightly influenced.

On the island what he had was like a dog, a very large happiness-creating dog. This dog was his wild, warm, positive personality.

He spoke some Greek. He could read and recite Ancient Greek. He was in some ways like a god, not a Greek but a big mild wild American god.

You could study Evan as part of a study of American divinity. His divine energy and gladness were not qualities that turned women off.

In addition to his real qualities, Evan, like some of the

Greek gods, was a great bullshitter. He tried to make girls think he was even more vital (and important) than he was. "I was saying to xxx," he said. Actually Evan was as good as, or better than, all the world-class people he so much mentioned and admired.

That they didn't mention him so often may or may not have been at least partly due to the fact that they were all so busy working that they couldn't be gods.

Evan gave his time to life, which is the reason we all wanted his knowledge about women—it wasn't quite what you'd call know-how.

Because Evan's information wasn't calculated to make you succeed—more to help you to understand and to avoid the worst pain.

Evan is lighting a woman's cigarette. He wants her to be completely understanding of and completely generous to him. Then he will reward her with the food of the gods: silence, talk, no children, love, a bemused and vague infidelity.

I want something more!

Most of what Evan says can be understood in the light of this situation.

They remember *everything*. And so on. There was something right about Evan's views of women, but there was something definitely wrong about them, too. Don't let them get to you, Evan says. Herndon can take Evan's advice when he is on the outside but not once he is starting to be on the inside of feeling in love. Then there is something so sweet that Evan's voice can't enter. Always, though, at such times, happy times, Evan goes along. Aren't they, isn't it, marvelous? he says. Dig it! When Herndon is thrown out, he needs Evan's advice. What can I tell you? Evan says. I am obviously the *wrong man* to tell you about *anything!*

LE JEU DE L'AMOUR ET
DU HASARD

On the porch of the hotel they sat and looked out at things they could see. They played a game. The father said, It is red but stippled, and they had to guess what it was. No that could not have been the game. He was sitting in an automobile four years later thinking about that game. Perhaps it was this: the mother said: I see three things beginning with an *L*. She meant of course in English not in Greek. Maybe that was possible. The child, a little girl, was at a certain disadvantage in being only five years old. She played along though, and of course the mother and the father made it easy. It was best when she would win. After they played the game for about half an hour, the mother took the child inside. Their rooms were on long corridors. Bathrooms were at the far, non-porch end. After a while the father got up and went in to his room. The mother (she was thirty-one) was lying in the bed. The father was thirty-six. He looked fondly at her and said, Did you like the game? She lied, Yes. Then she said, I'm asleep.

STEPS

The baby was walking up and down the steps in
Herakleion. These were some stone steps, part of a royal
or it may have been just a slaves' stairway, now mostly
destroyed, and most probably entirely destroyed and
now just partly reconstructed, of the Palace of Knossos.
The palace was dedicated to the Cretan version of the
Olympian gods—Apollo in the guise of Helios was a
prominent one. Here had lived the king, the court, and
all the utter craziness of Crete. King Minos, with his
Labyrinth! His annual sacrifices of beautiful boys and
girls! King Crazy, if you ask me, said Mollie, in the
bright sunshine, who was helping the baby walk. Up
down, down, down, down, down, now, now, here, down
up up up. The baby walks crazily, she is like King Minos.
She does what she does to make sure she can do what she
is doing. She, though, does no one any harm. Still, if she
had the power . . . ! No, her father thinks, as he walks
about trying to look at the palace and thinking of his
baby daughter at the same time. No, if she had the
power, she would be kind. But how can one be sure? A
hot breeze slapped him, then, dust in his face. From a
stair his daughter fell and she was screaming. Rapidly he
turned around to get her, and then he was like a god.

IN CRETE

I love you! the girl called up the slope of the small hill on which I stood gazing after remnants of a few stones of Crete. Well, I love you, too, I cried, touched and excited, though she seemed only about twelve years old, dressed shabbily, smiling very happily, there right next to her sheep. But, why do you say such a thing? where does this feeling come from? you've just seen me for an instant, since I got to the top of this hill. The beautiful sun shone down, and there was a breeze to which all shirt parts in response fluttered, and did, too, in its way, my smile, that was not so much fixed on my face as by the slight breeze being held in place there smiling yes tell me. The world is at peace, I thought I heard coming from the cliff. She then kept smiling, happiness-looking lips and teeth. She gave me a little wave. I know now she hasn't understood more than one word (maybe "love") of what I've said. Did some American, tourist or soldier, teach you to say that? I said. She picked up a little lamb and held it so I could see all over its fleece. Smiling, waving I was. She put it down, turned then turned back to me, giggled, waved, again turned and walked away. The world had been at peace for about ten years. Greece, though, was still full of (new) ruins and the terrible just about undeal-able-with feelings left over from the civil war. I stood there not in love but, I thought, aware of something in love that love had never brought to me. There didn't seem any reason why it should, although it was a possi-bility of life.

AGOROKORITSO

Agorokoritso, a rather badly made movie about a Greek tomboy who finally finds love, is showing at the one local movie theatre. Three persons are in this theatre, it is an outdoor theatre, though with the construction of an indoor one. That is to say, it is like a "regular" theatre, though very small, without a roof. One doesn't drive into it but sits in a row. The little girl went to sleep after five minutes. When she woke up she saw her father's hand on her mother's shoulder, his arm around her back. The movie had just ended.

The house they go back to has no running water. Water is pumped into a cistern by the water boat once a week and may be taken in bucketsful from there. How dry the climate is! though not too dry for ants. There are, what, maybe thousands of them in the white baked-clay-wall-bordered courtyard.

After watching them one day, moving around, the husband wrote a story, called "The Storm of Ants." In the story, he stressed the need for enduring suffering and going on with one's work, since suffering was bound to come anyway and work was all to the good. The main character was a young man who after successfully completing his course of study at the University of Athens, was caught in, defaced by, and shortly killed by a storm of ants—whence the story's title. He showed it to his wife, who said she didn't like it much, it seemed needlessly horrible.

Later, feeling restless, he found himself walking down near the theatre again. *Agorokoritso* was still showing. This time (he looked in and saw) there was no one in the theatre at all. The film and his story had no audience.

IMPENETRABLE LIFE

Two rabbits looked out from behind a rock. Robin saw them and looked away. He was waiting for Patrizia. He kicked a little stone. It skittered about ten feet away. The rabbits were startled and began to disappear. Disappear is not usually qualifiable, but what the rabbits did was to dart then freeze, which gesture they, like certain tribes of Indians, believed made them invisible. Then they started to run the rest of the way. Patrizia came up the walk. Robin ran down to meet her, and the rabbits, re-startled at what seemed this new direction of danger, began another sequence of disappearance, a sequence that actually brought them more into the view of anyone who might have wanted to harm them than they had been before. They darted here and there, and their day was full of disappearing. Big-eyed and excited, they ran around as if other beings existed only as avoidable dangers to themselves. That is why one could find them lovemaking, or eating some grass, later on in the same day, with the greatest calm, as if they were without any doubt at the center and the earth were theirs. Family organization was loose, and it had no social or political extensions. Each rabbit was on his or her own, like a stranger at a party, though a stranger who looks basically like everyone else. Robin and Patrizia's return, their walk back up from the rocks by the water, alarmed the rabbits again and brought on another sequence of disappearance.

WITHOUT A DICTATOR

The girl too felt sunlight on her shoulders as she stood among the stones of the "Altar of the Nymphs." The boy had gone there first, and now she was standing there. After he had been there a few, maybe five, ten, minutes, the boy had run down the steep hill from it like a sheep. A little lamb, maybe, or perhaps a goat. The girl kept standing there, though, and putting her hand on one after another fragment of stone.

Mussolini was happy that the Rhodes "ruins" had been rebuilt. Now the trains run on time, now man knows it is better to be a short-lived lion than a long-lived sheep, and now there are ruins standing again on Rhodes. The people say that under Mussolini, too, things were "cleaner." That they were nicer, as well as things being on time. On Rhodes, in fact, so far as Professor Shoates could see, there wasn't much that could either be or not be on time. It was hard, too, to figure out "nicer" and "cleaner." It was nineteen years after Rhodes had been liberated from Italy, and everything appeared to be both nice and clean.

His son has vanished. He's worried about that. The boy has a little history of being unbalanced. In the time of Mussolini, Sergeant Kanakatos says, you could be certain that you would have your son back with you before dark. But now there is a different kind of person, and less discipline, and we don't know. Katie wasn't frightened, just sort of in a vague mood of concern. Buddy's disappearance makes the island less clear to her in one way and in another more vivid than it was before. It was now a part of their own lives' urgency. Could Mussolini, if he could be brought back, really help, have helped?

Shortly after dark Buddy is back all by himself. Seeming a little perplexed, and also annoyed, at his family's concern, he said simply, as if that accounted for everything, "I met a girl." Katie knew it was not the one he had been at the "Nymphs" with, for that was she: so it must have been someone else.

ARTEMIS

I got out of the car. So did Delia. The wonderful, white Artemis statue was on our left.

Artemis served such a variety of roles in different phases of Greek religion that if you were to come up behind an Ancient Greek and suddenly shout Artemis! he would not know what to expect.

He might think he was going to die (Artemis was a goddess of death), that his wife was about to have a baby (she presided over birth, was a sort of goddess-midwife), that the moon was up, that he should look to his virginity—or to someone else's—that it was time for the hunt. These were just a few possibilities. She was beautiful, there with her deer or her dog. And shining quiver!

In her dress, with its stiff folds hanging down in straight lines from her shoulders, unbelted Diana! Later, she leans partway off a small vase that the Ceramics Museum was selling a three-dimensional copy of for so many thousands of drachmas that was the equivalent of four dollars. Can we get it? Delia asked.

Of course, I said, though I felt a pain in my left shoulder from saying it. Four dollars seemed a lot to spend on a little jar. Delia was my wife, and it was nineteen fifty-five and I had, but she had not, changed any money. While the young woman at the counter was wrapping it in newspaper, I felt weak. I-I can't buy it, Delia, I said. It-it costs too much.

Oh, Gilbert, Delia said. I like it.

But I don't have—   (She): Well, all right

I bought four little vases—gray, pink, and white—for

8000 dr. (about five cents) each, in part because I liked them and loved their being so cheap, and in part to make up for not getting her the other one.

From time to time I felt bad about being so cheap. Sometimes I tried to make up for it.

My desk faced a window, and on its wide sill stood one of the five-cent vases I'd bought in Greece. When I stood up, the desk bumped, and the vase fell off, down into the courtyard. We heard a tiny sound, "Ptootph." Delia was standing there, wearing her old faded pink dress. She looked wonderful in it. I should, I thought, buy her a new one.

What was that? Delia said. A little vase. Oh go and get it, she said. I probably can fix it. So I did. It was only broken in half. When I got back upstairs Delia was smiling. Listen, she said. I have something to tell you. I'm going to have a baby. Are you glad? We can afford it, yes? I hugged her and gave her a kiss. Of course we can afford it, I said.

Delia looked particularly beautiful when she was pregnant. She was the one who really cared for our baby, modestly and increasingly carrying her around. And after they were two separate persons, too. She almost died when the baby was born.

Artemis, in sculptural representations, was smiling, either because it was easier to sculpt mouths that way, or because a tradition of divine (including Artemis's) facial expression was begun by its originally having been easier to carve mouths that way, or—and this is the part that for us had all the interest—because she is full of some secret happiness that we can never know. Why is she so happy? Delia and I discussed it. Artemis certainly wasn't cheap. She spent everything she had at every second, living, as she did, in the midst of an infinite supply—not of money but of power—like all the other gods. Could that, along with sweeping self-confidence, be what made her smile? Delia thought not.

We were drinking ouzo. Delia had on a pleated white dress, and when she stood up, she picked up her light raincoat as if it were a bow and arrow. A Hellenist we knew, who I think was in love with Delia, said that sometimes she made him afraid. Delia thought this absurd. Bob would look better without a beard, she said, about him. He had a brown one.

He came calling. In some ways he was better than I was, but Delia didn't love him. He would certainly have bought her the vase without hesitation. I was glad she didn't love him. I was afraid that without her I might be dead.

The problems with this story are several. One is that it is set in the nineteen fifties, when (1) Artemis was no longer a real force in the world, certainly not recognized as one except possibly by an Artemis Cult somewhere, and (2) the marital customs, the relationship between Delia and me, have acquired a distracting "period" effect that threatens to be more interesting than what I mean the story to be about: my finding of Artemis/Diana—with her powers of death, childbirth, chastity, the moon, the hunt—in my modest, shy, intelligent, midwestern, upright, cool, blonde American wife. Reading the story up to here elicits comment on the "fifties relationship" the two of us had—I changed money and Delia didn't, I made the decisions, she cleaned up the house. We had to live sometime. It might as well have been in the fifties. There—look! It's fifties! Fifties wine. Still, you drink it and it makes you drunk. Whatever the epoch, I was drunk on and mystified by my wife.

Hello, I said, when I met her. She was standing in the same big office I was in, at the University of California, in Berkeley. The hills were foggy in the distance. Bees, and other less useful insects, jumped up and down and around in them. Oh, Delia, I said. What an inter— what a beautiful name. My glance traveled around her. A man came into this office, and a woman left. The desks stayed there. A goddess, I said, rather foolishly, in the Berkeley T.A. office (Delia was another of the names of Artemis/Diana). Well, she said. A few days after that, we went out together. We drove into the hills and parked and kissed. Later Delia was willing to make love.

young
We loved each other and were ignorant.

Gradually the Dianahood of my wife-to-be possessed me. Delia gave me all the things I didn't know I wanted.

She wanted something, too, she told me, from our making love. "I want to experience evil," she said. "I've never done this before."

THE MUSIC OF LIVES IN BED

In the middle of the night (it was about five a.m., their middle of their night) he asked her to turn over and reassure him that she was not gay. She thought that was ridiculous. She had been his mistress, then they were married, and now they were divorced. Why would they still be sleeping together if she was homosexual? She thought, I won't even bother to ask him that. Why use logic to dignify this idiotic conversation? It was this sort of misunderstanding, of unwillingness to talk, that had broken up their marriage. That, and his foolish, over-anxious, unself-confident questions. Now, it seemed, though they were back together, they were starting to be detached from each other in the same way. I hate her, he thought as he shaved on his way to making her breakfast. I detest him, she hummed as she pulled the top sheet up to the top of the bed. She is loathsome, he whispered inaudibly as he set down the coffee. He is a horror, she barely murmured as she lifted the cup to her lips. I want to go to the movies today, he said. Let's go then, she said. And feeling various ways about each other, they went outside. The day is chilly, there is a little rain. She takes his pleasant, reassuring, reassured arm and very silently says Phhhhtff!

A SENSE OF THE TRAGIC

The Dutch have no sense of the tragic, Charlemuth said, as he and Georges and I gazed at the seemingly happy folk of Delft riding on bicycles, sometimes even wooden-shoed, garbed in blue and red, hilarious. No sense of the Tragic at all. My days then were wonderfully untragic as were my nights. The nights were clear and as if blown away, or at least blown clear by every passing day. June was wonderful. June was the woman I was with. June combined beauty and kindness with an incomprehensible fondness for me. In the great industrial suburb of life we had found each other. Each of us looked for a sense of the tragic. Soon the Chinese may become just like us, Michel said (some months later). I said I doubted it. Under the stars everything was clear, like Byron's club-foot. If only they had named it something else, Byron said; but the English were unsparing: they called them as they saw them. You wouldn't find them eating herring, wearing blue white and red, and wooden shoes, and riding about on bicycles. Not the French, Charlemuth said, either. His poetry was always so sad. Clouds vied with azure and stone to accomplish miracles of solitude and darkness. Willows wept. And night broke clear of them all. June decided, after a while, that we should be married. She wanted to have children. She wasn't tired of ramping around but she also wanted that something else. I was hesitant. I talked about it to Mack. Don't have children, he said. You're right. It's completely unnatural! Don't you think you're going too far? I said. No! he said. For emphasis, he stopped the car. Holland was far behind, far away. No, I mean it! Eventually I lost June. Mack, Charlemuth, and Georges were still around.

RELATIONS

At twenty-six, one night in Paris, I dreamed that my parents came to visit me. The dream had the vividness of an hallucination. There was shuddering and shaking it seemed throughout the hotel. My mother said, "Kenneth!" Her voice was loud and intimate at the same time. Then my father shouted my name, too. They both appeared at my door. A little snow was falling on the rue de Fleurus. Busses had stopped running hours earlier. An occasional car was still able to move easily through the beginning snowfall. I sat up with terror at the sound of my parents' voices. The snow kept falling, though it didn't fall more heavily; and, after sitting up and staring, getting over the dream, then walking around the room for ten or fifteen minutes, I lay back down to try to sleep. I would have left my room and walked a little ways through Paris but for a peculiarity of my hotel, the Hotel de Fleurus. Once ten p.m. had come, you could open the hotel door from the outside but not from the inside. If you were in the hotel you were in for the night. In this respect, being there was like being a child.

I wrote a poem in this hotel room. I wrote several poems, but none worked out. The one that I liked was really only part of a poem. The four lines I wrote were written three years before I had ever seen Ekaterina. I was not even a graduate student at this time. At this time I courted Sonia and Gilberte and Anna of the dark smiles and eyes, Anna of "I don't know how to kiss." All this and all these were far far from the "I do know how to kiss" of Ekaterina, and the "I know what follows after" and "be careful, you are playing with fire" to which I replied, stupidly, "what else is worth playing with?" Ekaterina was a moderately tall blonde woman in a candy-striped green-and-white dress in an undergraduate class at Rutgers, the same age as I was, twenty-nine. And, soon after meeting her, I finished the poem, with my subject now having appeared, after so long, starting with the lines I wrote before—

> Oh what a physical effect it has on me
> To dive forever into the light blue sea
> Of your acquaintance! Ah, but dearest friends,
> Like forms, are finished, as life has ends!

AN ADVENTURE OF THE
FIFTH SENSE

Tommy grabbed hold of his hand as they walked out of the school's little auditorium, where they'd seen, along with Tommy's sister Annie and his mother Chloe, who lived with Mike, the film in which Mike played an important part. It was secure to hold on to Mike. His image had been on the screen like a true image. Much mysterious affect was to come after this, but this was that. The city (Paris) lay stretched out before them like a huge laundered but unironed shirt. So many fluffily white passages and uneven trails. But Mike was Mike, this was safety in one big number, and Tommy holds his hand. He has very small fingers, but for Tommy it's hardly a question of a small hand (his) and a large hand (Mike's). They are, the two hands, completely different, so then how can each be a hand? About fingers, nails, palms you don't make a judgment. You hang on. Chloe is far from being jealous. She has Annie's little hand in hers. And so the City of Light is navigated today. People who would have been of no importance in the time of Louis the Fourteenth are now the object of attention. Even their slightest feelings are the object of attention, of the most intense and serious kind.

PLANNING LIFE

They'd made an agreement (his idea, poor goof) not to make love. Each understood that this was just for a while. After this time they would devise something, neither knew what. Fond of him, she took her blouse off but this was before the agreement. He went to adjust the stereo, through which Bach was coming penetratingly clear. Blue white cloud on azure green photograph sky. Vienna and Rome. Places. The arch of your left foot. So forgive me. Oh silly, he said. He'd found it terrible not ever seeing her. But now what was he going to do with his collection of desires, the desires for her, that he wasn't going to fulfill? When they made love for the first time again, she fainted. She felt the excitement of a walk of which she didn't know the end—adventure, wandering. In America, a nineteenth-century French writer said, *tout est chemin,* everything is a path. How could she not go everywhere she could? How could he not, too?

LIBRETTO

A friend is coming to dinner, the friend he would like to set this text of his to music. Henry, a middle-aged man, who had lost his daughter when she was a baby, owns and operates a gas station somewhere in the American West. To this gas station comes a young married couple, Bert and Matilda. Their car has broken down, and there is no place but this one where it can be repaired. The mechanical problem is serious and takes Henry several days. Henry and Matilda fall violently in love. At the moment they are realizing that this is so, a car drives up for gas. In the car are a man and woman and a small child. the young parents sing a duet that begins:

> Fill up our gas tank with Texaco
> We all are driving to Mexico

Their revelatory conversation interrupted, Henry and Matilda now look at each other in a startled way. The sight of the young family in the car has brought them what seems to be a memory—of intimacy, of a voyage, of a loss. Aren't you—no—could you be—Henry stammers. And Matilda, Oh no! My daughter! Lost, in time long past! No, cries Matilda (Louisa), no! But yes seems certain. The lovers' union cannot take place. Arias are sung, cried, whispered. The fear of incest prohibits them. There is no consummation. Bert and Matilda (Louisa?) leave, she full of the ravages of a forbidden love. Henry, as the automobile's sounds fade, sings, whispers really, just one word: "Louisa!" Two: for then: "Matilda!" It may, after all, have been a mistake.

He finished the libretto around five o'clock. At seven-thirty, Alfred arrived. This young composer is American and has been living in Paris. He read the libretto. Ellen said, Here is dinner! It's beautiful, of course, Alfred said. But I don't think it would go over in France. The French would find it incredible that they didn't even make love once, since they don't really *know* if they're related. Oh you've been staying over here too long! Sean said. He was offended. He wanted the breakup to seem a necessary thing.

The year before, before marrying Ellen, Sean had fallen in love with Louisa, who had a husband much older than herself. In the libretto the older man was the lover and the young one (Sean's age) the husband. In reality it was the other way around. She also fell in love with Sean. She said to him, they were on a bus together, I can't leave my husband and my son (he was five years old) in any organized way. I don't have the heart. But if you will take me, I will go with you right now. Sean said, Wait. A while later it ended. Sean despised himself for what seemed to him his cowardice in not having taken Louisa for his wife.

The libretto wasn't set to music. Composing, for Alfred, was more a wished-for than an actual pastime. What he really loved to spend all his time doing was playing the piano. He went on becoming famous at doing that. Sean died young. The apartment where Sean wrote the libretto was torn down and replaced by a condominium. Alfred has a carbon-paper copy of *Louisa—or Matilda,* the only copy of it left—but it's missing the last page. A composer who long ago heard of the libretto now wanted to make it into an opera. With no copy of the end of the libretto in existence, it is now possible that the story could turn out in a different way.

Three persons are eating oysters in the Café du Dôme. One of them, twenty-eight, the youngest, is smiling, and it's not only the wine that is making him high. He is full of the pleasure of a libretto that he is "taking over," getting into someone else's skin to write. His new contribution to it is to take the events that have happened since, and the secret details he has found out concerning its composition, and to make that all a part of the libretto. The new text delighted the composer, who wrote a beautiful score.

Louisa! Matilda! Applause, applause! Ellen comes to Paris for the world premiere. She is wholly carried away by this opera. Like several others in the audience, she is part of the story. In Bayonne, New Jersey, sat Louisa, who didn't know about the opera and who wasn't there.

HOTEL LANCER

An angel flew in the window, of fine fresh sunsplit air, so rare in London, and they both turned around. They had been quarreling by the open French window, from which you could see the river. The quarrel began in a discussion of the plan for the day. The mother wanted to go someplace and sit (and write postcards); the father wanted to do some vigorous touring. He had a list. The quarrel now was about what each of them wanted to get out of life. The little girl sat crying on the edge of the bed. When she was born, the father sent a telegram to his parents: Charlotte fine and Baby Helena into the bargain. We send you love. He telegraphed, at Charlotte's request, to her mother too: Both girls brave and beautiful your baby and ours. They decided to take a boat ride on the Thames.

GILBERTE

1

Gilberte, restless in her limited modernity, came from the provinces to Paris and was rather silent there. She came to the crémerie in the evenings, after her restless afternoons. Je suis étudiante en droit, she said in her fairly low voice. Gilberte was unhappy, or, as she put it, she had "les idées noires." This was the fate of almost every aristocrat in Heian Japan. Despite the just-about-continuous sexual activity and the most refined aesthetic behavior ever seen on earth, the Heian were pervaded by their fateful knowledge of the Buddhist philosophy of history, which placed them in a hopeless age. There was no way out. Gilberte tried to drown herself but stopped. One evening she turned on the gas in her apartment, but a window was open. At twenty-five she finished her studies and became a law clerk. She went back to the provinces to see her parents. She remembered, as it happened to her again, how helplessly she started to stammer when they were around.

2

I was immediately interested in this particular girl because her name was Gilberte. This was because of Proust. We both ate in the little crémerie, I suppose there has never been a really big crémerie, on the rue de Fleurus, in the block between the Luxembourg Gardens and the rue Madame. Gilberte and I joked around. I was happy to know enough French to be able to talk to her.

She seemed glad of my acquaintance, as odd as I must have seemed to her—a tall, skinny rather clumsy American (this is 1950), and always joking, in a language I didn't entirely understand. She wasn't exactly pretty. She had the trace of a moustache and rather dark skin. She wasn't especially happy either, nor joyous, nor what is called full of life. Sometimes she seemed very sad. If I asked about it, Gilberte would tell me that she had "les idées noires," the black ideas, dark unhappy thoughts. But what did I know? Gilberte's reality ended for me with the wall of the large building that held her tiny room (I never saw it, she never invited me, or permitted me, in), there to be succeeded by her irresistibly seductive reality in the pages of Proust. So I was puzzled by the actual Gilberte time after time.

Reading her letter, saying she was sorry but she no longer wanted to see me, I was, as I had often been with Gilberte, on the corner of the rue de Fleurus and the rue d'Assas. The afternoon shadows hanging from the corners of buildings were as dark as my first image, before I knew what she meant by them, of Gilberte's "idées noires." I felt a sharp pain in my abdomen and in my chest. I might really never see Gilberte again. I was twenty-six years old, Gilberte was not my first love, and, actually, not my love at all. Though I was reading *Remembrance of Things Past*, I did not at that time understand how horrible the life in it was. I felt its great variety, its nobility, its sensuousness, and its heroism, and I wanted it to be mine.

WAGON-LIT

The wagon-lit was rumbling. Trick tracks climbed up through snow-mountainous night. His hand is on her thigh but someone else is speaking. She just felt sexy. Later on she would rebuild an important museum, and then when she thought of this night she would think, That was not me really. I was not myself. Meanwhile back in the Unreally somebody if not herself is essaying to lie partway down so her new acquaintance here can be inside her to make love. The train lurches, it's not easy. Soon the bright dark light of Paris is staggering over them all. Swaggering. The Gare de Lyon collects them and flings them out into Paris while it is snowing and neither one can find a cab. A taxicab strike, which is not really itself, has just about immobilized a great portion of France's capital. Whoever thought we'd breathe this fresh spring night again? he asked his friend. She smiled and said, I have to phone Marie. Tonight she was scheduled to arrive in Paris. What happened on the train? In Italy the coffee tasted good. At every moment, as he drank it, he was thinking of what would happen later on. She didn't mind him, but that's the way he was.

THE ALLEGORY OF SPRING

The blossoming cherry trees were quarreling. She thought this when she was fifty yards away and when she was closer, right in amongst them, she imagined she heard them. One tree said to another: I am prettier than you. And the other said: It is impossible for you to see yourself. But I see you. And I tell you you're wrong. The first tree disputed the illogic of this remark. And so on. She went on walking, and when she came out of the cherry grove, she had been through a lot. She hated quarreling. Dietrich was standing by his boat. Come, can you go out with me? he said. I don't want to quarrel, she said. He didn't understand. Well, will you or not? he said. Yes, she said. Then she said, No.

BORDER

At the border the French customs person, a woman, seeing the baby, Charlotte, two months old, swathed in
white, smiling, and transported in a basket, commented
"Quelle Calvaire!" What a Calvary to have to travel with
a baby. Whereas moments before, far from confiscating
anything or delaying them at the border, the Italian customs crew, two men, had untiringly chucked the baby
under the chin and exclaimed about how beautiful she
was. The baby grew up and liked Italy better than France
but not for this reason. Deeper and underneath this and
all similar reasons was the passivity these Americans
showed—you could call it, if you wished, receptivity—in
regard to the voiced opinions of the Mediterranean
working class. Deeper than this, even, was the instinc-
tive—or old-civilization-induced-become-almost-in-
stinctive—wisdom and grace they assumed these Mediterranean people had. Deeper than this were the
groundwaters of which the Mediterranean itself would
be formed, one fine morning when the chill wind blew
over from the Atlantic and the hot from the Sahara, until
the rocks and bitter thyme and pollen said, "Here we
have a sea." Boats slavishly crossed it, for millennia.
Charlotte was born. She who one day standing on the
jetty felt the terrifying shocks in her, like cannonfire and
not too distant, of motherhood and love. Whereupon
another tiny infant could become the subject of the Sol-
omon-like decisions of the sun-tan-faced people who
kept working all the same. Che àngelo! Tesòro! said one.
And Ah M'sieu Madame quel cauchemar! (What had

the Mediterranean to do with this?) said another. Butterflies, yellow and blue, groped up the white cliffs almost never reaching the top. We have to ask you to open your bags, said the man in Italian customs. All right. She held onto his arm because she was always frightened of customs. You may close it, please. The baby was screaming like a car accident. Bon dieu, Good god, said the French customs, can't you get that little monster to be still? The baby also was named Charlotte, and she grew up.

WHITE NIGHT

Moon shining on Dan. Who said, He likes you almost as much as I do. Therefore. A party again. Scotch and soda, orange juice, marc de champagne. In a garden of tilleuls were broken. They sat around, raspberry juice. A few of the lives were in a state of being broken. Tears would follow, and shaken heads. Chins would be raised in sad determination. Those who were lucky would love again. Some craziness would be dissolved. It was too bad for this one and not so bad for that one. Have a glass. In the glass was something. It changed the way you felt and were. Alcohol, that simple hand, pushing you to this and to that. But it will never find her. The man needs the woman he will have to fight. One is a slob, aloft and away from his feeling. He wants to be a doll. She wishes to be a dog. It has to be gotten through. If it is not love, is it convenience? If it is not convenience, is it Dan dreaming really? This happened very fast to be happening again so soon. He has gotten a bit closer. He reaches for her hand. She showers him as with moonlight with a smile. But this smile is to please her and is the last he will get, for a while. Later, there will be other smiles, in other places. How did they get in this position that so encumbers and burdens their hearts?

One night in Barcelona, he said something. And then she felt something and she said something. But what had happened before that? Back and back and back it goes to their attraction the first time. He has something that she needs. She wears a slow white dress. Close up, they are finding the most of reality in satisfaction of an infantile wish. This thread led him to this party. The minute hand was turning. The second hand was broken. After a long while, there was the sun.

A DOUBLE STANDARD

A man walked into the public baths, and after a few minutes a woman walked out. Inside the Baths the man was asking about the price of a towel. The woman at the steamy little desk told him what he wanted to know and pointed to a hallway of tubs each protected by a door. On the doors were steamy edges, vapor drops, little squiggles of water that leaped and stood up. He opened one and he hung his towel inside. In moments he was naked. A moment more and he was filling up the tub. The water boils, it manifests a mighty gurgle. He turns the knob and stops its flow, puts in one foot and then he sinks into the tub entirely. The woman walked out into a sunny day. An automobile was standing in the street. Like all women, like all men, she wanted to be loved. For some months now she has felt that this is not happening. She is young, she has no humor about it, she needs to be reassured. The man who is taking the bath has no idea. She is wearing a dark green blouse. He is not her man. And she is not his woman. But he might as well and she might as well be. For this bathing man's woman is thinking the same things of him, and she has no humor about it either. The two women, one in a light yellow dress and the other now running across a park, dressed in green and whose eyes are dark blue, will decide this matter. The gray statue in the park has a curve of rock to its hair. When the man gets out of his tub he seems larger than usual, because he is in such a small room. Later that night he is diminished. He breaks a window, he even tries to break the bed. She will never come back. That god-damned bathtub, that god-damned fool that I was! The second man's wife, on the other hand, relents; he remains temporarily—maybe even permanently—ignorant of the way things are.

ON HAPPINESS

It was distressing to think that Kawabata had committed suicide. It wasn't distressing, however, to find out that he had defined happiness as drinking a scotch and soda at the Tokyo Hilton Hotel. An acquaintance of mine thought this was a terrible thing to say, to such an extent that for him it seemed almost to destroy the value of Kawabata's work.

Sitting on the terrace of the Hilton!

What's wrong with that?

A friend of mine, a woman, once explained happiness to me.

We were sitting in the Place de la République in Paris, an unlikely spot for happiness. We were tired, had walked a lot, had sat down at a large, generic big-square café. Dear though it may be to its proprietors and its habitués, it seemed ordinary enough to us. So we sat there and she ordered a Beaujolais and I, a beer. After two swallows of the beer, I was overcome by a feeling of happiness. I told her and I told her again about it later.

She had a theory about a "happiness base." Once, she said, you had this base, at odd times, moments of true happiness could occur.

Without the base, however, they would not.

The base was made of good health, good work, good friendship, good love. Of course, you can have all these and not be "happy."

You have to have the base, and then be lucky, she said. That's why you were happy at the café.

Kawabata asked my acquaintance in turn: How would you define happiness? He told me his answer: "I said 'How can anyone answer a question like that?'"

THE LOCKETS

It's just the worst kind of weather, he wrote to his fellow poet and friend, for writing poetry. But when he came home, he had a marvelous long poem. He had been telling the truth about the weather. It was cold clear and still and it didn't inspire him. One day, though, he started to write *The Lockets*. He felt good because he had been patient enough to wait for a true poem to arrive. Usually he wrote a poem all at once, but this one occupied his time for day after day. By the time he finished revising it, it had been almost a month. This seemed to him a very long time but also a very short time, since if the poem was as good as he thought, it was a lifetime possession, a place, as it were, like a country house, in which he could live whenever he wanted, a place full of sunshine and clutter, comfort and surprise. The weather he hadn't liked was in it, but transformed by words. There was also a certain irony in it that sometimes he thinks he would have liked to leave out, but that is the kind of person he was at the time. Most of it was like a big, cold, frilly place by the water, decorated by someone else (Poetic Tradition?) in a more elegant and fancy style than he could have found for himself. He wanted to show it to his friends. He was sitting now in a room on West Eleventh Street looking at one friend reading it who seemed almost shaken by terror because it was so good. It might have been, in fact, since the friend had a cold and a slight fever, that he was shaken momentarily by a chill. But the sunlight filled the room, and what did it matter? He knew that his poem was good, and that his friend, whether he thought so or not, would tell him that it was, and that he would believe him.

NOTRE DAME AND CHARTRES

Of the three young women standing in front of the cathedral, one was worried about her sexuality, another
was in the midst of a probably destructive love affair, and
the third, who was so far a virgin, was blind. Nora did not
use a dog to help her to move about. Today, she was with
her friends, and in any case, she had been blind for a long
time and had developed a sure sense of place. She carried
a cane. For Catherine, sex was good and sex was bad—of
course, in different ways. In a way it was the summum
bonum and the happiest thing in her life. Leaves
swirled—taken up by the autumn wind as a waitress
takes up her apron—across the parvis, the forecourt, of
Notre Dame. Women, in her secret belief (this region of
her secret belief was in some respects like a small-town
library containing random books in different sections,
some in Religion, others in Mechanics, Physiology, Politics, Literature), women did not feel overt sexual desire.
When she felt such desire, she felt she was less a woman.
Never admitting to her sexual feelings, even when they
were very strong, she would allow herself to be surprised
by them, and give in sexually to the most inappropriate
men. She was unable to talk about this situation with her
two friends. Denise standing next to her was intent on
pursuing a sexual passion to its end. The man, object of
her desire, was rich, married, arrogant, much older than
she, and unfaithful (even to her). He had a pleasant voice
and dark blue eyes that, each time she saw him, seemed
to pass like a long needle or a hat-pin straight to her
heart. He had a certain way of touching her, carried over

from his profession (he was a doctor, an internist). To patients it was reassuring; to her it gave an impression of sureness and strength. These two were describing the right front doorway of Notre Dame Cathedral to Nora. Three days earlier, they had gone to Chartres, and there both Catherine and Denise (to their surprise) felt jealous of Nora's enjoying it so much. Clearly much more than they. Only human relations cause that much joy. Nora's was from the kindness of her friends—as attentive to her as lovers, and two of them at that! She was fascinated, at both churches, by every detail.

LIFE AND ITS UTENSILS

"Life and Its Utensils" is at the museum. A song runs toward us with its poster. It is the sun! At the museum, the utensils are arranged according to use: here a knife and fork and platter and chopping bowl and a neon sign saying KITCHEN, another saying MANGER. Here are some dark blue paintings—the utensils, it appears, of Waking up. Here are the seams, the pins, the pink roses and yellow cellophane thread that are the utensils of Summer. The weakness of the show is its disorder, its incompleteness, the evident fact that the user of all these utensils is not here.

The use for things I find (I think) when I am with you, O perspicacious heavenliness. That's you, over here, with me, now over there, whiskey, a summer flatness, a winter's snow, oh you're the one, who is saying, Green crayon, green crayon, green crayon, who knows what coils are in your heart?

When we came out of the museum, nothing was the same. That is, for a couple of seconds. Everything looked like a utensil: the hill, for supporting the sky; the sea, an electric knife for slicing the sunset's cake, etc., etc. In another museum, there is a show entitled "Objects: Lost, and Found." A very large blue mirror is just inside the entrance door. Looking at it, one sees into it, as is the case with mirrors, and there is nothing in it at all. That is the Objects-Lost. The rest of the museum is filled, I mean really genuinely filled, with objects found—everything, gloves, engines, canisters, barrels, flowering plants, love manuals, she-goats, backgammon boards, coffins, fat people, seeds, everything that could possibly, ever, in a lifetime or two, be found. The trouble is there is no room to walk in this museum, no way to see, except from a distance, most of these exhibits, and going into and among them, a person becomes one of them him- or herself.

Space travel is gone, Leaves of Grass is gone, Bonington is gone, Delft is gone. All that is left on this highway is a couple of trees. Under them a car, that is, it turns out, a little museum. "Life and Its Dashboards" inside. If you're not distracted by this, I am. The life of anyone shows how happy one can be. And how unhappy.

We found in the Museum of Words, a man who had never taken a wash. He was all alphabet, from head to foot. From foot to head laying him sideways he spelled DEUS RERUM AQUEO (God is the water of things?) and reading him head down it was A NEW SILENCE. We couldn't speak to the man, so we went away. Prose and her handmaid, Poetry, followed us. The Words Museum had many other shows. I was alone. I sang a song I had known from other cultures:

When man alone
Suffers enticement
Greece overthrown
Rome's no replacement
A railroad terminal scudded with snow
A lovable scene designer's elbow
These will all fall under the knife
Of the Utensils exhibit of life!

After I had locked my song in a neighboring window, I walked out onto the museum promontory to smoke a glass of blue air, when suddenly, you (the woman in question) come back in sight. Where've you been? Gerard Manley Hopkins is gone and filigree is gone, filigree effects are gone. Here's the Summer Wind Museum, with its technology of throats.

And the Museum of Being Permanently Closed. It isn't a museum, it's a mortuary, a coat for old friends. You were startled by being in your coat. You startled me.

The Power Museum is gone, and the Hooks Museum is gone, and the Life Itself Museum is drifting away. The French have hysterical blindness, the Italians depressive moods, the Spanish what? Hesitation about being around.

You'll admit that it's been quite a day for going to museums! A medium-sized amphitheatre now, filled with car wrecks, would, for this twenty-four-hour period, be sufficient to round things off. A young school-teacher (Andy?) who lives in these parts is tagging along with us, asking questions: Do you like our country? Which show did you like best? What, according to you, is the most significant for our time? Oh, all of them, Andy, all! But it would be great to go swimming! The Museum of Oceanography is right here. Great sharks pasted to the pinewood, corals hiding beneath the timbers of the floors, mermaids and mermen dancing attendance, and everywhere the mysterious artifice of salt. After this , finally, we go home, to the non-museum of sleep.

THE RESTAURANT ON
THE BEACH

In the Trattorìa della Toscana e del Mare, clamshells
and the "sounds of the sea." Shellfish—clams—by the
dozens and dozens were being devoured. Pick up slip
slap slurp clack jangle back onto the plate. A woman had
a pain in her jaw. A man, a lover or her husband, placed
his two hands gently on her jaws and eased them a few
times open and closed. A mother and daughter had
hardly spoken to each other for a year. A year in such
circumstances is a long time. Napkins flew in and out of
the diners' hands. The girl finally found it in her possible
feelings to forgive her mother. At the table their hands
crossed. The mother seized the girl's two fingers and
held them. A bare-looking beach, flat, not generous with
its sand, though furnishing a base of hard sand for whatever sand might be added, though it would be sturdy
sand that could resist the breeze but above all the waves
that, small and low as they were, periodically came all the
way up, just about to the edge of the Trattorìa della
Toscana e del Mare, this beach was brightened by sun
and by the sun's reflection. Automobile horns honked,
but just a few, on the half-kilometer-away road. The restaurant from the outside seemed only a shack, but it was
comfortably set up inside. The mother let the daughter
drive, a relief to them both.

JULIAN AND MADDALO

The young Englishman and the equally young Italian nobleman were riding in the latter's carriage on the out-skirts of Venice. They continued their trip in a gondola, from which at a certain point a little island could be seen, with a building on it with a belfry. The Italian told the Englishman the building was a madhouse. Somehow from this began a conversation about the Christian faith, about whether it was possible to believe in it or not. The Englishman said it was not; the Italian said he found it amusing how passionate (and persistent, he had known him before) the Englishman's feelings on the subject were. More momentous than what they said or did seemed the beauty of the end-of-the-day Veneto sky, a pale bright splendor of pinks, oranges, and golds. Hav-ing been tired but with their tiredness now turned to tenderness by this visionary loveliness, the two friends descended from the dark gondola at their respective homes. The next day the Englishman went to call on the Italian nobleman. The latter had not yet risen, so the Englishman took advantage of the time to play with the nobleman's daughter, a beautiful, sensitive, intelligent child. Her eyes, he thought, were like twin mirrors of the Italian sky. They gleamed, however, with the luminosity and intelligence that one found only in the human gaze. He was sitting with her, rolling balls about, on the floor. When his friend was ready, the two men set out in a gondola once again. They continued their conversation, now bolstered by the passage of time, and by the events of the night and the morning, about the viability of the

Christian faith. Their plan was to go to the madhouse on the island they had noted before and, once there, to talk to the "madman," who turns out to be not at all mad, though a man who was, years before, temporarily driven out of his senses by the reverses of love. Voluntarily he had confined himself to an old tower amid the isolation of the Adriatic isle, and then his strange ways, which consisted chiefly in his unusual wish for solitude, caused people to think of him as eccentric, even mad, and to begin to call his tower the madhouse. The two friends hear all of his story. It enchants them. Christianity and its problems are forgotten. Each of them—they are both profound lovers—feels close to the madman; with a common desire they ask him to return to the mainland; they will help him, financially and otherwise, to set up a new life. No, thank you, the madman said. No, I cannot. And in this perhaps, only, but perhaps not, he was mad. Finally, their kind offer kindly refused, and the dark night coming down, Julian and Maddalo go home. The eight-year-old girl is called to dinner. The "madman" waves to them. Later he falls, stricken—by some malady of the heart—his painful life at an end.

A MOMENT IN THE LIFE OF
ANNA TAGLIAVANI

Windows slammed, doors opened, and she walked into a place where there were banks of drawers. A note left out on a filing cabinet fluttered to the floor. Bending to pick it up, she saw a white folded dinner napkin hanging on a very low railing. First she picked that up in her hand and then went after the note. When the entire area was clean, even spic-and-span, she closed the doors, opened the windows to let in some fresh air, looked out at the canals—there were two of them converging where she could see—took off her dusting cap, dried off her hands against her apron, smiled, and twirled around. She did a little dance, a sort of tarantella, then opened one door and, going out through it, resumed her place in society once again. This "cleaning lady" was a talented dancer.

Anna, there is an opening at the theatre. Gerolama is ill.

A little more cleaning work, then, for money. And hours and hours of exercises. She had done them all along.

She even did some housework the last possible day.

Off slipped the apron and down threw the cap, and the broom is replaced by a wood post on which she leans, breathless, about to take her first longed-for (tanto) leap onto that stage. In midflight she imagined herself cleaning, and, for an instant, she looked about, to see what was there. But by the time she landed, that phase of her life was done. She might clean, a little, now and then, in secret, but she would dance (it seemed decided) for the world.

ELBA

They lay on the beach.

While they lay there, the sun came up.

This means that they had been lying on the beach all night.

The beach they were on was not anonymous.

It was the beach Napoleon had landed on when he was imprisoned on Elba.

It was a beach that was a moment in history.

Napoleon, landing there, was unaware of this beach as "beach." This is not so now.

Now it is Napoleon's beach. How can it be anything else?

However, this endless life of tourism, of conquest, of idealization, of adventure, of going "out of oneself," to what can it lead but murderous disappointment and depression? You only think that way sometimes.

At other times, you love life, you love this beach.

Lying on it, you may be covering with your body the sandy places where once Napoleon put his feet.

If nothing else were happening in the world, this would be a little something. I admit that it's not much.

However . . . what do you say to a night on Napoleon's Beach?

All right, I will!

AT LAMBARÉNÉ

From the ocean came a light and salty breeze. It made a
delicate light film around everything it touched. Sick
persons were arriving, sick persons were getting better,
some sick persons were dying. The sea rose with a sort of
wail at Lambaréné, and after a very hot, close "taxi" ride
through the bush, on jagged bumpy roads, Lopan got
out, stretching his limbs and straightening his sleeves, he
was wet, from the heat, and went walking in, expecting,
almost, to see Dr. Schweitzer himself. Schweitzer said,
The death of an insect is a significant death to me. It had
been hard all Lopan's life to live in the shadow of Dr.
Schweitzer. Miracles, he thought, might still happen in
the world, but probably not here. Schweitzer had done
whatever could be done, and in its turn this initial inspired miracle was now the scene of the humdrum of
accustomed failure and success. An old woman, maybe
eighty?, attracted his attention. She was sitting in a low
chair in a room with a poured cement floor and with
half-opened curtains of brush grass between her and the
view of the sea. She was softly singing (there were inter-
ruptions for coughing and sometimes what seemed like
gasping) a traditional Fang song that Lopan knew. The
old woman reminded him of his mother, who, he
thought, might have been offended at being compared
to an old sick black woman in a hospital in Gabon. On
the other hand, maybe not. It was something to him that
there was no relationship—he could, at whatever time it
pleased him, move on. He left the old woman and
walked about—looking, asking questions, saying polite

58

things. He too, of course, was a doctor. After about forty minutes, he walked outside to the cab and told the driver, who was surprised that he had come at all and that once there he hadn't stayed longer, that he wanted to go back. The driver was a Mpongwe. Like the Fang, the Mpongwe were a tribe that inhabited Gabon, though far fewer in numbers than the Fang, and who, unlike the Fang, so far as Lopan knew, had never been cannibals.

ON THE SAVANNA

The zebras, like the wildebeests, are always on their toes, so to speak—alert, anxious, sensitive, worried-looking. Some distance away reclines a lion. These elephants, though, seem relatively at ease. They have an air about them that they are the only ones there. I don't think they're worrying about lions. The elephants are vegetarians, and like vegetarians everywhere they know what's right. What's right for them: trees—Wham Gark Thank You Bark, Heave Sleeves Thank You Leaves. The elephants are going at it, an independent centrally-willed group that feels its identity so strongly as to make it feel safe. The elephants are not only centered and living by rules, but they are *big,* too, and have tusks and a trunk to go along. An adult elephant can handle a lion. A baby elephant cannot. The babies, being possibly edible, are connected to the rest of the savanna. A little older, they are too strong and too tough. The mothers close off the appetitive connection as much as they can. At first sight of a lion, a baby is surrounded, and the lion goes off, its mind already on other prey. The elephants' isolation goes on as before.

THE CLIMATE OF GABON

In the brush nearby there were only small animals. At the
Hotel Rampinadanda, Madame Oubala is writing a
message down. The stamp is too big to go on the card!
What a laughter from the back of the lobby and some
students were staying in the hotel—students in France,
dans la métropole, though teachers here. Among these,
Hervé Blanc. Mme Oubala lifts up her pen. The message is written down. The blazing white-pink sunlight
fills the lobby air with a tuneless sort of illogic, as if it
were the eyes of a great animal, whose hide and claws
and horns were the trunks and suitcases that are beginning to be dragged down the stairs. Hervé, though he
would have liked to stay in this what-could-seem-for-
an-instant paradise of early hotel morning, has decided
not to stay. The young women who work in the "casino"
are still in bed, mostly sleeping. There is one whose hair
in disarray she is staring down at the distant swimming
pool. And shaking her beautiful head and hair, she says
(to Jean-Simon), Hervé is leaving today. Did you know?
Jean-Simon rises from a pile of white linen and stares
into the hotel room sky. Could you give me my glasses,
please? he said. She did and also took up hers in her
hand, and thinking of Hervé's going they both put their
glasses on. He has a large property in France, he told me,
Sylvia says. That's nonsense, Jean-Simon said. Jean-
Simon was right. Hervé does not. The sunlight is getting
very hot. Hervé was thinking: I have to go back because
my life isn't going anywhere here. Could I take Millie
with me to France? "Hervé is leaving, as I always knew

he would." The sun is very high now, blazing, though it is cool in Sylvia's room. For a while, there, she and Jean-Simon go back to sleep.

HOTEL LAMBOSA

He closed the university down, she said.

There is nothing like being in the middle of a seduction in a strange country in an unfamiliar hotel.

Especially when one has known the person who is its object for only about forty-five minutes.

Being "inside" this person was a kind of enchantment.

Each instantly had the feeling that the other would be lovely to be with in a bed.

This feeling turned out to be true, and the strong, swift sunlight cluttered and clouded their room with pennies of the future and nickels dimes and quarters of the past.

When he got up to pick up this money, he saw that she was there.

She was lying on her side, gazing at him.

She said, So now no classes for a while!

ACHILLE DOGOS

I

The African (a Zairian man) spoke, sang, recited, wept, laughed, talked with amazing rapidity. He was performing, for a large audience, but specially in honor of me and a few other visitors to Zaire, a work he had created about the politics, excitements, anguishes, and ironies of World War Two and the years just after. He took all the roles himself. At one moment he was Churchill, at another Eisenhower, at another de Gaulle, and so on. He was Hitler, Mussolini, Stalin, Konrad Adenauer, John F. Kennedy, and all the other leaders of the wartime and postwar world. At the same time he was speaking, crying, and singing, he darted around the room, turned his face, adopted different poses, lowered his head, threw his hands in the air, fell flat on his rear, scuttled across the room on all fours.

A good many of the connections of the act were made by puns—Hey ha ha, where you build a church? It's up on a hill, that's why we call it Church Hill! (Enter Winston Churchill) Did I hear my name? Going to strike the animal, strike it where it sleeps. We have to Hit Lair! Ho ho, speak. (Enter Adolf Hitler) Well I am Hit-lair. Who now says my name. If then when my friend feels not so strong, he'll lean on me. He must lean on me! (Enter Benito Mussolini) Ho, I am Benito Must-lean-on-me . . . Once introduced, all these characters acted out the wartime and postwar doings of their respective nations. This included the lead-up to the war, the invasions of Poland and of the Low Countries, the Blitz, Dunkirk, America's entry into the war, the Russian front, Rommel versus Montgomery in North Africa, and so on and so on. The conclusion was an impassioned plea for peace by John F. Kennedy. At the end of it, the performer fell down as if shot—many spectators screamed—then got up as himself, Dogos, and bowed.

This performance lasted about an hour. I applauded with all the strength I had left. The others on the podium applauded as well—enthusiastically, for a long time. I was weak from what he had done. I was also frightened, given the applause, that he might do it all again. He didn't, though. Instead, he bowed, graciously (the applause continuing), then walked over into a corner to talk to a friend.

2

The Churchill part was hard to figure out, but at last he got something that resembled (in Luba) an upper-class British accent. Adenauer was easy, the German accent was. American was hard, French was hard. Italian he thought he could fake. It was fun to figure out what the people would say. It was more than fun, however, his act. It was complete involvement for him and total exhilaration. It gave him the feeling that in his body—in his temples, his shoulders, his neck, his strong thighs, in his abdomen, and in his vocal cords and mouth and throat—he had the entire true history of World War Two and the period after—this period so important for Africa. Period of independence and struggle. And of good leaders so hard to find.

When ready, he went to present himself, with held-in feeling, at the Nomakin granary door. He had once or twice been in a real theatre but it was usually in a place like this, made into a theatre for the occasion. There was one he now thought of, outdoors, on the Esplanade by the river, a rough place, dangerous to act on, littered with sticks and pieces of stone. His performance there was one of his first; after that, usually, he asked for a place indoors. The granary was crowded with spectators. He took a long breath, concentrating on imagining himself to be Churchill, and walked in—to board-thumping, screaming, and thunderous applause.

3

Achille Dogos is walking by the River and he is listening to its sounds—Agounaboupaboumba. Here is the idea for a play all in one phrase. A goon named Boup invents a kind of music he calls Boumba. He plays it and thousands come to hear it by the River every night. In *français* the *Fleuve* says *un-con-aboup-aboumba,* more or less the same. Well, is a goon a *con?* Achille has yet another idea. Of course. And this idea is the River itself . . . Congo. Or else, modified by the sound he had heard it make, *Con-*Goon. The idea for the play is now clear: *The Con-*Goon: a collection of foolish actions performed by one French and one American character, both of course acted by Achille. The Congoon. All the sounds in it will be the actions of the two fools.

4

Achille Dogos was puzzled when he received a copy of Edward Paunaman's long poem *The Lockets*. An American passing through Kinshasa had met and liked Achille Dogos, had thought he might like and profit from a little avant-garde American poetry, and sent him the book. Achille read it with great difficulty (it took him almost a month), and when he finished it he immediately began to work on ways to act it out. With the first ten pages, he did pretty well. He liked what he was acting, he thought he was feeling in his body the freshness and violent activity of the text. The long set of stanzas about the different kinds (some fantastic) and colors of subway cars stymied Achille for a time, but not for too long, for he found a way to get down on all fours and slide back and forth while shouting them out. The slight narrative thread of the long poem—it was a parody of a nineteenth-century British girls-cum-aviators-book kind of romance—delighted him and gave him ideas for many things to do. That, and the grand, very grand, climactic whirl of the conclusion, which left him sprawling and exhausted, spread-eagled on the ground, or, when it was indoors, on the makeshift stage.

The piece, for the wild energy of its performance—and given Achille Dogos's already-great reputation, the love and esteem of which he had for a while now been the object of in Zaire—this enactment of *The Lockets* became a "hit," and a standard part of Achille Dogos's repertory, wherever in his large country he went. Almost every educated person in Kinshasa had seen it, and many rather simple and uneducated persons, too. Still, when Edward Paunaman won the Nobel Prize, Achille Dogos didn't hear of it. Nor did Paunaman know anything about Dogos's performances.

Persons crippled by polio are permitted by the government of the Congo to go with free passage on the ferry boat across to Zaire and to bring back a certain amount of merchandise without paying customs duty on it. Many things not available in Brazzaville may be found in Kinshasa, and the helpless persons (mostly men) have great trouble making any money and satisfying their needs at home. Thus, this is a compassionate law. The boat, almost every day (it crosses the Congo once in each direction every twenty-four hours) carries a surprising percentage of passengers in wheelchairs with crippled limbs. One of these, to his delight, has found someone to wheel him to a rare daytime performance by Achille Dogos. Forget, he thinks, the duty-free merchandise. He has to—the performance lasts all day. And he must be back in the Congo by dark (the ferry leaves at six). Today's show is a special one—a gala performance to celebrate the election of the new Premier. Or, rather, of the same Premier but from a new election.

The sun shines on Achille Dogos's body, as for the middle section he hurls himself to the floor and begins the passage of the "underground trains." This passage, to the cripple, Mouno Agoba, seems the very image of his sad and twisted life. For the first time since childhood, he bursts into tears. Paunaman, could he have seen this, might have struck at his heart with his hand and not known why it was there.

THE HEART ATTACK

I had a, well, a thing with a very important man, she said. An industrialist. Lived in Zaire. We were. It was a man of fifty-eight years. That would have made her at the time sixteen. We were happy. Last year he had a massive heart attack. Not quite dead but the affair was over. He was enfeebled, weak to the point of bed rid. He lies on a couch, exhausted. He cannot move his arm. Frédérique. But his servant does not hear and does not come because. He is living. Oh but for me it is as if he is dead. Tales from Africa. This man was the bridge from her sixteenth to her eighteenth year. It had, too, to be in the "colonies." That kind of power and isolation in the Métropole does not quite exist. The chief confidence everyone had who had the strength and the leisure to think was that the situation in regard to money and power would stay in place. An ornament, a decoration of this status quo was she who came like a gilded butterfly to pose on the stark dark arm of the man with two billion francs three years before he was going to die. His wife is in an elegant room taking care of him. The French are the cleverest people in Europe. This continent is dark but its sun is bright. The man, dying in Africa, very frequently thinks about the girl. Her father was a friend, in the Ministry of African Affairs. "If you make her happy—" He put his hand on the girl's father's shoulder, who without being able to help it, slightly recoiled. His heart attack finished it really. I had to leave Africa. At that point, everything was impossible.

AMBROSE BIERCE

When I reached my hotel room, which was on the twenty-second floor of the Hotel Rapontchombo, from the windows of which I could look down, in the daytime, at the tiny naked breasts of the wives and daughters of French residents of Gabon lying sunbaking at the pool—they excited me, perhaps even more than such a pleasant sight ordinarily would, because they were just at a distance to make them resemble in size, and thus for me in remembered splendor, the tiny photographed breasts of the Folies-Bergère girls on the rough ivory-colored and sepia brochures my mother forty-five years earlier had brought back from France—in any case this time, this night, when I got to my room, I saw something horrible: lying on my bed, a torn-off arm spattered with blood. It held down a piece of paper on which was printed, in large letters, *To Professor Koch, from his most appreciative students at the University of Gabon.*

There was a story behind this kindness: it had to do with the American writer Ambrose Bierce.

"Their favorite," the coopérant Jean-Pierre said to me while we walked along in the heat and even a hot breeze, ouf, and the lizards, I telling myself every half hour at least whoever it is was crazy telling me that Libreville was wonderful, beautiful, "Paris by the sea." The best thing I've done here, I thought, is get a second kind of malaria pill to take in addition to the other one. Favorite—Jean-Pierre was teaching American literature at the University—American writer is Ambrose Bierce. Why? Well, his stories of the supernatural, of magic and horror, seem like just plain truth to my students. It corresponds to their view of life.

I was in Gabon to read my poems to the American and English literature students, and to discuss poetry in general with them. Several times in their questions they brought up Bierce.

Bierce's stories are filled with ghosts, disappearances, mutilations, acts of magic, all varieties of weird events. One poem of mine I read was "The Magic of Numbers"; this poem interested the students far more than anything else I read aloud or said. In it I used the word *magic* somewhat ironically and fancifully as one might in a phrase such as "the magic of Italy" or "the magic of a kiss." They, however, taking me at my word (magic) hoped they might, in penetrating the poem's secret, find out something of use.

Thus the arm, the bloody severed arm in my room. It wasn't really a human arm, but something that looked an awful lot like one, a pretend arm that some gifted craftsman among the students had made out of papier-mâché, bamboo, and paint. The arm was to show their opinion that I was of the high order of American writers that included Ambrose Bierce. I knew the world of spirits.

At least this is what one of them—Kabamu—told me the next day. We were standing on the Rapontchombo Hotel "breezeway," where the air was completely still. What he told me made me eager to see my students again, to talk and think about all this—I liked being regarded as one who knew the spirits—but there wasn't time.

Oh well, I had the arm! I would take it with me and read more Bierce. When I got to my room, though, in the last hour, ready to pack and to leave, the arm was gone. Of course, it would be! On the bureau in its place was a note, signed by the whole class: "Professeur, bon voyage!"

STREET THEATRE

What's bad about Italia, Maria Teresa said, is that you do something buona nobody notices it. But you steal the rear window from a car, eh, if you steal that, eh, quello è bravo!

My wife and I were startled. Yes, of course. *Bravo* meant, and it had been years that we had been using the word at the theatre at concerts and at the opera, *bravo* meant "good."

"That had never occured to me before," I said.

"Well, yes," Maria Teresa said. "It's evident. That is what is wrong with this place."

She came to live in America (in New York). Nobody said bravo about anything except in a theatre.

Ten days afterward I went out in the morning and looked at the car. Its rear window was gone.

It had been perfectly, meticulously lifted from its rubberized frame; not a fragment, not a scratch. Niente. Nothing. The May wind came in.

Quello è bravo, Janice said. In America there'd be glass all over the place!

SEA

The sound of the sea is:
1) illusory
2) not noticed
3) noticed but not cared about
4) cared about for a practical reason
5) cared about for a general, poetic, artistic, or life-center reason
6) ?

No matter whether perceived or not, or how it is perceived, the sound has the same reason: the boom thrut thrum of the impellment of strong ocean against bashed tides by leavings trials and leanings of wind. So a child becomes a poet and is impractical. He never learns how to use the sea. So a child becomes scientific and eludes its suggestions. Together they both live however in a world that includes (and importantly) the sea.

How do you like the ocean this a.m.? Beautiful, isn't it?

Ranging from a velocity of forty miles an hour . . .

*R-R-R-R-R-R-R*oar *rush* rush . . . . . . Sfooroom . . . .

I found a quarter this morning lying in the sand at White Peach Beach.

Show it to me show it to me show it . . .

Taking it she touched his hand and that day, affectively, was over.

The next day there were still a lot of battered-looking barques on ocean surface.

Life does nothing to change it. Does it change us? It is, we obviously are, different from it. Proof:

possession of ears, a mouth, a nose

Insofar then as we can talk about it, everything (except the real problem) is solved.

She is excited to be spending so much time in the salt water and in the sun. If only he had known how little time he was, comparatively, putting into his (psychological and emotional) investigations of her salt-slaked body. The ocean was making a noise that was in no way a reminder, and was completely unpolitical, too.

A political movement resembling the ocean should be thought about only on a page.

It keeps reminding them of health, and in a way, too, of love and delicious sex.

The sea is neither masculine nor feminine but a great gross encourager of both.

By the time she had the ideal view of it, for her it was too late. And that was true of him, too. Nonetheless in the absence and in the ill of it, in the near-missing and in the concussion that was in reality too the confusion, they went on hearing it and being approached by it, from time to time, as if they were in such control of it that they could stroke it and make it roll, contented, away.

The resort closes. One more season! Or one less! A note is pinned to the door:

NO CATS

NO HELMETS

NO BILLBOARDS

NO SOUND OF THE WINTER Z

PROHIBITED!

And not even in the evening do they or any come back.

END OF THE DAY AT
ALABIALAVALA

The French always made us wear these "colonial" hats, said Mrs. Ribaviabala. She smiled, almost laughed. We were sitting down to lunch, white tablecloth. For some rice water? Oh thank you yes. Mrs. Ribaviabala a rather elegant lady. Rose white dress. Dusty two of us Americans are from the road. Nice you to have us. Oh yes, Mrs. Ribaviabala said. Pleasure our. Drank we and ate we very nice. To I have made a translation, Mrs. Ribaviabala said, these for you some of our Malagasy verse. I then thank you, she me them handed. White sheets of paper clouds in sky clear above Alabialavala. The poems do not say much. Nor to judge by these translations are they very advanced in technique. But the ambiance nostalgic of that Ribaviabala! It's her giving me the poems translations harmonies! I will read them in the speeding car. Dear Mrs. Ribaviabala, Thank you for lunch. And thank you for the poems (translations), which were good to read. He did read them or he does not, says Mrs. Ribaviabala. It seemed a polite man. So often though Madagascar Europe American people do not what we want. Even when it is promised. Mr. Ribaviabala walks up from the garden with a cricket in his hand. Saying, in Malagasy, "Look at this!"

SAINT-JOHN PERSE AND
THE SCULPTOR

The sculptor worked.

The jungle—bush, really—was around him, and the sculptor worked. He said, Dis-moi, Chef, to the tourist there. He said, Dis-moi, Chef, why are you come here to Gabon?

The tourist had come there to see a woman he loved. His love was composed of several factions. One faction wished to see him dead. Another wished to raise him, victorious, above the sea.

I don't understand.

Dis-moi, Chef, qu'est-ce que tu fais ici?

Now you are beginning to sound like Saint-John Perse.

I met him once at a party.

What did he say?

Oh he was very much like this sculptor.

Covered with dust? half-naked? twenty-two years old? and working on a false folkloric head?

No, of course not.

Dis-moi, encore une fois.

The dirt, the dust was swirling.

Henri had to find Catherine by eight that night. Vingt heures. After dark it wouldn't, probably, be possible; and the next morning he had to return. Oh well, why did he have to return? His job, his law practice, his living. But wasn't this the living that really mattered? He turned to the sculptor. What? Perse said, What is it that brings you to this gathering? And the young sculptor—"Chef, qu'est-ce que tu fais, donc, ici?"

The answer to both was love—incurable, unsatisfiable love, rephrased as (to Perse) I wanted to meet you, and (to the sculptor) I wanted to see the country. At the reception for the famous writer there had been Jeanne, the attaché's young wife. Now Catherine was in Gabon. Both answers were true and false, as both questions were genuine and insincere.

THE LIFE OF THE CITY

The whole city could be seen reflected in the surface of the rectangular flash bulb of his Canon AF35M II. Or at any rate, that of it which seemed to him significant. There were the old city wall and the first line of buildings. And there was the sky with, piercing it a good ways to the left, the white spire of the Cathedral. City, church, and nature were represented there. His wife had an automobile accident and broke her arm. His daughter was once again mended, after falling off a horse. His own health was excellent. Of the city there were both the political, governmental aspect, represented by the wall, and the private, familial aspect, represented by the buildings, which were houses. His daughter had been arrested for dealing drugs. His wife was under the care of a doctor, for alcoholism. He himself was dying of merely having been alive—for eighty-five years. The camera was gone. The city wall was still there, but many of the houses were gone. They were replaced by enormous "high-rises." These buildings were colored a darkish yellow, mainly, or a dark pink. That was nice, he thought. He wasn't really very old at all. He was going to meet his wife for the first time, at a dance in the Old City. Inside the city walls a few old buildings were, apparently, crumbling, but he was young enough to not even take care as he walked past and around them. The young woman was lovely. The spot where he met her was covered by a large shiny pump.

A BUS

The Muslims would not eat seafood and did not eat pork or drink wine. A seaside bar-restaurant in the middle of pig country would have had, here, little success. Yet this was not such a place, but rather merely a place in which to drink tea. The tea was sweet and had sprigs of mint in it. On these sprigs, as often as not, there were bugs. Ira looked at the bugs but drank the tea. The word *assassin* comes from the word *hashish*. Groups of men were given hashish and verbally inspired with wild dreams, then sent out to kill the victim someone wished to be dead. Hashish was differently esteemed in a culture where no one could drink alcohol. It could be regarded as the only "out." The "in" was to drink the tea, which Ferrabonzo found "molto forte," very strong. He looked at Ira, considering him as someone he might speak to, but rejected the idea. Ira had fallen asleep. He was very tired. Ferrabonzo slapped a few coins on the table, stood up and went out into the street. There a camel brushed against his shoulder, leaving traces of straw mixed with dust. Ira woke up. He didn't want to order more tea. Several of the bugs had crawled up out of his glass and moved lazily across the table. The bugs looked more repulsive out of the glass. He was sorry now he'd drunk any tea. He thought if he drank a bug it would give him a disease.

His wife smiled at him. She had stayed awake. Their daughter, who had been asleep on her lap for a long time, was very small. Don't worry about the bugs, she said. They won't hurt us. Beepie, Beepie, wake up, she said to the baby, who, however, continued to sleep. Come, sweetest. Daddy has to pay and then we'll get on the bus.

The large, filthy, dark yellow, wheezing bus had just started breathing harsh breaths in the street. The driver came out of it into the relative cool of the café. Ferrabonzo was already on the bus. He had decided to go on to Elizir. The driver called out, in Arabic, Anybody for the Elizir bus? Ira was nervous and the baby had just started to cry. A brisk whiff of hashish seemed coming from where the bus driver stood and a largish man was pushing his way off the bus. This was Ferrabonzo. It all smells of hash in there, he said half to himself and half to them. To ride on it doesn't seem safe. Although each carefully guarded his or her individuality, in such a situation as this, thrown together by a portentous circumstance, they couldn't help talking together. The driver hesitated at the door and on the first step of his bus, noticing that now he had one fewer passenger than when he got off, and that two (three including the baby) very likely passengers were making no move to get aboard. They were, instead, indeed, all walking away. So be it. He went up the stairs and into the driver's seat, conducted his foot to the accelerator at the same time as one hand to the wheel, with the other on the starter. Then the bus smelling of hashish smoked by a previous passenger sped away. This possibility—regarding the hashish—occurred to Ferrabonzo, to Ira and to Helena, at the same time. Now they had seven hours to wait, with no prospect of much that was agreeable except sitting around and dozing and drinking tea. To their pleasant surprise, however, the bus came back. The driver had forgotten his purseful of change, which he'd put down on the counter in the café. Unsurprised, ungratified, uncurious, and truthfully, a little dazed, he watched the three (plus the baby) formerly-supposed-secure then supposed-lost passengers laughingly and excitedly getting on the bus.

IN THE LOBBY

When she came down she found him talking to the manager of the hotel. They had, it seemed to her, developed, for such a very short period, an extraordinary intimacy. Each man in fact had this "intimacy" close to the surface all the time. It wasn't exactly "intimacy" but a volatile personality substance that could turn into it on contact, by means of speech, with the air. From this intimacy she felt somewhat excluded. Too bad. He had a far finer substance ready for her, made up of all that he had ever felt, secretly felt, and thought and seen, and which, on contact with her person, with her talking, her mere aspect, turned into love. It did this when he saw her now, and his closeness to the manager faded. It faded quickly. The woman, seeing him so engaged there, had walked outside. He followed, and there on the porch were three women, between medium height and tall. One was the woman he felt love for, but for a fragment of a second he couldn't tell which one she was. Understandably. In fact it was three shining images created by the blindingly blazing sun. She was all three. As, shielding his eyes, he walked toward her, she laughed and said, How did you get so close to that man—in such a short time? I was surprised when I came down. Did you get the bill? He had paid it, and they put their bags in the car and drove off. He would always forget that moment and always remember the one of her telling him she was surprised. She said things about him that seemed to be praising in him some virtue, but later he felt she had possibly been ascertaining a fault.

LES ONZE MILLE VIERGES

Saint Ursula made sure that every one of the eleven thousand girls she took with her on the expedition was a virgin. A non-virgin would have ruined the perfect symmetry of the population of the expedition, have made the titles of paintings or verbal accounts of it complex and difficult, and could, too, have exercised some kind of bad influence on the other girls. Why are thoughts like these in my head? Eleven years ago, after learning that a friend of mine had unexpectedly died, I went out and walked through the city "inhabited by buildings." This phrase is Pasternak's, for Venice. I went (it was nearby) to the Accademia to look at Carpaccio's Saint Ursula paintings. At the harbor, in the boat, again on land, silvery, yellow, orange, blue, were all the Virgins, alive at first, then massacred, laid out flat. On each slain one was a speck of red. The most stirring pictures were those of the Virgins in the boat. Heading, heading for somewhere, for a Good Destination, they all stood facing in the same direction. My friend didn't paint subjects like Saint Ursula and the Virgins. He was far from doing so. He painted friends and family members, though the way he painted them they seemed to have a kind of innocence, even a blank and optimistic spirituality that might be associated with the looks on the faces of the Carpaccio girls. That is, if anyone had ever wanted to make that connection. I can see eleven thousand of them—Jimmys, Johns, Annes, Lizzies, Katies—all shining with blankness and enthusiasm in a boat. Not on their way to martyrdom, but there, posing, on their way somewhere, even if only into paint.

CITIZENS

One cloud had gone away, and then another. Pretty soon
the sky was a clear light blue. No, there is still one tiny
cloud left there, toward the horizon. Dominick was sitting down staring at his shoes. They were big army shoes
with dried mud on them. He was trying to remember the
words to a song he had sung when he was fourteen. No
use, though. The words wouldn't come. Dominick was
eighteen and had nothing to do today. He stood up, feeling the ache in the back of his knees, and walked toward
the Siracusa town line. In ancient times, Siracusa like
other Greek cities had not been a closed-in place. You
could be a citizen of Siracusa, a Siracusan, if you lived
twenty miles from the center of the city. Whoever came
in to Siracusa to vote was a citizen of Siracusa. Walled
cities were a later invention or the invention of different
civilizations. Like Athens, like Sparta, like Corinth,
Siracusa as a political unit was not geographically confined. It hardly remembered being Greek now. It remembered and it did not. There were fragments of walls
and a fountain, the Fountain of Arethusa, which was
actually Greek water with around it an Italian low wall.
And there was a tablet made and incised in twentieth-
century Sicily to explain what the "Fountain" was. By
now, Dominick was pretty close to the fountain. When
he got there he again sat down. He traced figures in the
dust with his right forefinger. This good-looking tall in-
dolent boy was the favorite of his mother, among her
eleven children. Dominick threw a pebble at a bird but
he egregiously missed. The pebble hit a wall and the bird

went rapidly off. West of there, about five streets away, was a balcony surrounded by fence wire on which an idiot or at least someone out of control of her life was moving back and forth, able to take the air in safety because of the wire. This unfortunate, fenced-in girl was Dominick's second cousin, Lucìa Caranotti. Her condition, in Siracusa, was believed to be untreatable, without cure.

POLENTA

He really loved the polenta, and so did his friend. Next to it, on each plate, was rabbit. Wild boar might have been there, too, but wasn't. Wild boar sauce was on the large flat noodles three-fourths of the way up the hill in a smaller town. It was also on the broad flat noodles in a small tabaccherìa-con-trattorìa seemingly hung between two peaks of mountains, farther south. When the four terrible-looking men walked in, another friend of his had said (and how the wind was blowing—you'd think the whole place was going to come unattached and blow off), I hope we're in an Italian movie and not in an American one. If we're in an American one, we're really in trouble. The first polenta preceded an opera, and the female singer was a wonderful new star. She was going to be a star. Now she was first being recognized as a potentially great singer. She too ate polenta and was indifferent most of the time to her own eyes, mouth, and breasts. The first friend didn't meet her, and it would have been nothing if he had. In her career she was too busy. Well, it might have been something. You never can tell one hundred percent. The cold wind blows and the people want polenta. She moves among the chairs onstage, almost breaking them, waving her arms, head thrown back, she is singing. Afterward she is alone and in tears. That would have been his moment to come there. But he was in a restaurant, having some polenta in order to taste a certain wine. Heavy, a little heavy, but good. They went to see the opera the next evening. And they talked, they were so delighted with it, in the car, all the way home, and even further on into the night.

THE TANGO PALACES

I am going with my wife tonight to the Tango Palace! There were five "tango palaces" in Beijing. These were large roomy spaces in the enormous underground network of air-raid shelters built to protect the populace from nuclear war. Abandoned now, they constituted, burrowed under the crowded city of Beijing, a good deal of almost livable space. There was, however, a limited supply of air. And it was cold and damp, inconvenient for shopping and for other aspects of normal community life. It was true that certain things could be stored down there, and certain things were. There were problems, though, of rust and rot. It was no place for a zoo! Unappetizing for restaurants, as well. The dampness, the lack of air and, too, the lack of light made the shelters a problem to use. For dancing, however, they were all right. The snapping sultry sounds of a tango poured out into the dusty Beijing air. The government had come to a decision that was rather amusing, if sometimes hard to understand. Might not there be the risk of being questioned, or even arrested, while trapped there underground? This didn't happen though. Hao Guang and Ming Pei and the others there with them simply danced. There was enough air, with a nearby entrance left open, for two hundred couples to dance for several hours. After that, they had to leave.

It should be explained that in China, "tango" is a more or less generic name for a relatively slow and in-each-others-arms (up to a point) dance. Some of the music played in the palaces was actually tango, but most not. The word "palace" is also used oddly, to designate a special place of instruction. Special after-school art schools for children, for example, are called "children's palaces." For a reason known only to some part of the government, after twelve months the tango palaces were closed. The "ten entrances," as the passageways down into the shelters were called, were sealed up. For a while on Saturday nights guards stood at them, guiding people away. No more dancing. It's finished; the air-raid shelters are closed. Hao Guang came past with his wife, dressed and ready, after their one-hour bicycle trip, to dance, only to find such a guard. News of the closing had been in the paper, but in a note on the back page they hadn't seen.

Eight years later, the inhabitants of Beijing were told to get rid of their dogs. This, for most, meant killing them, since very few had relatives or friends in the countryside to whom a dog could be sent. The dogs, the government held, had to be eliminated because there was a shortage of food. With the people on strict rations, it was ridiculous for the dogs to be consuming meat or even rice. So every dog in Beijing, except for a lucky few was killed. The most humane method of killing the dogs was by injection but for many the serum was difficult to get, so dogs were drowned or shot. Some had their throats cut.

This might have been a good time to revive the tango palaces. Though the practical-minded Beijingese are not sentimental about pets as many Western people are, still there was sorrow in many houses. Dancing could have been a pleasant distraction.

The reopening of the palaces was possible. The gas emanations that had been detected in them were a problem that could be solved. Bringing the dogs back to life, of course, was not possible, though starting a new dog population was. Neither policy, however, changed.

PLACEBO

There is a pharmacy in downtown Beijing that sells, among other products, deer-horn powder, promoter of longevity. The government leaves this establishment alone. The people who work there can sell, and the customers can buy, all the ground-up deer-horn powder they want. As for the efficacy of this remedy, no one knows. A pharmacist says, Well, a lot of people use it, and they keep coming in for it, that's a sign it's doing something, they are still active enough to walk, and they're still alive. It's true that it's hard to know if they would be also if they didn't take it. No one has tested it against a placebo. Bright blue yellow and white original-painting advertisements for products were shining on the pharmacy's walls. A customer came in for the powder—the old man, who had taught physics at Beijing University, was white-haired and just vaguely bent over. He paid for it with crumpled bills from a worn-out pocket. That night, the pharmacist assumed, he would be riding high. Much better than with a placebo! he thought. The bent old man walked home. He lived in a dark low small nineteenth-century Beijing one-storey building in the midst of many others much the same—this was good housing for Beijing—about fifteen minutes away. Once home he put the package on a table, hung up coat and cap, and pulled the shade of his one window all the way down. He went to a corner of the room and what seemed to be a box, but was actually a cage, in which a tiny toy Chihuahua was trembling. He took it out and stroked it for a while. Then, holding it gently with one hand, with the other he showed it what he had brought. The tiny creature wagged its tail. He put the dog down, got a spoon from his kitchen cabinet and put one spoonful of the powder, with some water, in a little dish. This concoction the very old, completely illegal dog lapped up, then went to sleep on the old science professor's lap.

PING-PONG

Ding Wei slaps the ball hard and it falls on the far left edge of Song Jia's side of the table. Song Jia returns it with a slice so that it lands, then spins, then scarcely rises from the table on Ding Wei's side. Ding Wei lunges for it and just manages to lift it up so that it goes above the tiny low green net, but Song Jia is there to smash it, into sports oblivion this time, and the point is his. What you want to happen may happen but may not happen often enough. If you win, you will go to America. If you lose, you will stay right here. Life will be hard, but you will live. There are the pleasures of family. But for excitement, for travel, and for your country, it will be far superior for you to win. Ding Wei and Song Jia know this but only one of them can win. This is the last day of the Shanghai Divisional O Yun Dong Hui. Ding Wei holds the ball in his left hand. He is ready to serve. After the game, Song Jia goes out to walk along the Huangpu River. The night air is soft. In the river's surface the shining lights are like his shots—that white light there traveling to a black water wall, and this light, light white one, hung in the middle of a wave. He plays the last game over in his mind. Ding Wei also thinks of it. The difference from their last match, which he had lost, was so slight. As if physically moved by this thinking, he gets on the plane.

A SONG OF PARTING, OR ZHAO FAN AND I IN THE CAPITAL (BEIJING)

The furniture parts of the market were hard to go around—you had to face right into them like furniture yourself. No one here but fur/Niture allowed! their song seemed to be. Later, after a narrow ride, there are very cheap dumplings on the Forbidden City outside. It is astounding how little there is to do, so Zhao Fan and I decide we'll go visit some old house or houses in an un-known-to-us quarter in fact maybe doesn't exist. Get this, we're sitting in this box on wheels and a bicyclist is pedaling us around. This's called a bikeshaw or some-thing like that it's passing

> Extremely quickly
> If it is still
> Here/there at all
> Whoomf! it's vanished
> And now a bird call
> And it comes back
> Such is fate

I remember when I used to think I had a fate. Now two chances in ten of dying, one and one-third of going in-sane, one tenth of one percent of going blind, and so on. It no longer seems like fate. My destiny is done. Here's what happened: I wanted to be a ball player. I wanted to be a cartoonist, like the person who drew Maggie and Jiggs or Skeezix. I wanted to be a Poet. Then why my homodiecidigithrop are yez now writing the prose? I can't help it. I am a poet and something in me cried out: Prose. Write fiction! Go to China! Eat sleep! How can one eat sleep? Zhao Fan is wearing a thick brocaded dress. Snow falls on the Forbidden City, as on the market. No one expected that.

THE LONG MARCH

On the Long March, Wang Chuli said, during our rest periods, we read Whitman to each other. Which passages? I asked. Oh, I don't remember. Some of them are very grand. I tried to imagine exhausted impassioned aching goal-driven soldiers reading (or listening to) "I am he that walks with the tender and growing night," etc. Well, possibly. But I would like some verification. As to my getting on the plane and thus out of Kunming, "It depends on the weather," the agent said. "If it is over sixty-seven degrees we cannot accommodate you. If it is under that degree, we possibly can." I don't comprehendo. In the plane there is an expansion when it is hot, and it can take on fewer pounds.

In the few days before the plane would leave, I was with Xiao (Young) Li and the American girl, in the southwestern Chinese weather. The Green Lake Hotel lay all about me like a novella by Henry James but with one important exception—as far as my glance might reach, I could see no aristocrats. The Minority Nationality Girl, quite attractive, was no exception. Like the panda, even when at home—here my thoughts were interrupted by an arrival of Chinese friends.

They came, in an organized way, as a group. I myself had always cultivated a gift for aimless lonely wandering that gave no more pleasure than it gave pain, it gave a little of both; for aimless lonely wandering one had no one to blame but oneself. One couldn't say, If only it weren't for this damned delegation! Or Long March. I like the name Long March, as I should have liked, I thought, the name Big Breakfast or Endless Bath. But already my friends were in the lobby, looking for me. I was right there. Hello! What's up? I looked at my watch.

We've been sent to take you to the airport, Wo Lo said. Climb on the truck.

The American girl was turning into a subject for a novella—or perhaps for a poem by Gerard Manley Hopkins. Why not forget the general public altogether?

This American girl was one who, if things went right for her, would have a good influence on the world. She is passionately attached to the "environment." Not the theatre nor cosmetics nor the world of medicine or law had anything to say to her as fascinating as what was said to her by the environment.

The environment, after all, is just the place we are; it's what's around us, I said. What's so important about that?

Knowing that I was joking, she bared her teeth. You'll see, she said. You'll see. Meanwhile Xiao Li was buying, as he later described it, his first "Western" coat, a suit jacket, thready, gray, for about four dollars, on the street, in a stall. An enormous sum, really, for him, but still, a new wardrobe, at least the beginning of one.

Do you think the marchers really could have been interested in Walt Whitman? I asked the girl (Louise Farnham). Louise was nineteen years old and Xiao Li was surprised we weren't married since we spent so much time together talking. It is not Chinese but strange, he said. I would have thought it stranger for us to be married. I was fifty-nine years old, living with someone else, and didn't find Louise attractive enough to make me want to change my life so as to spend it with her. She was pleasant enough to talk to, but there was not, I thought, any prospect, even, of the "admiring excitement of union" (Auden's phrase). I seemed to get more of that from wandering around and being alone.

What a joy, though, sometimes, to talk to somebody! As Ruetta said to Bodge in Paris, At last! somebody from New York! Or one panda sees another one on the beach (improbable). Could the Chinese marchers have seen Whitman that way? How should company be cultivated? Good-bye! (to the group) I am on the plane. The true subject of the novella: people being together and being alone amidst the "environment." The plane starts moving. We're in the air.

THE GUIDE

My husband wants me to take the veil. No, I don't think it would interfere with my work. There are some women guides who do it. However, I don't feel ready for it yet. Maybe some day I will. Probably I will. She spent all the day or most of the day talking about Horus and Hathor and Anubis. The lotus is the symbol of the South and the papyrus of the North. Nervousness is nothing to her. She seemed a complete stranger to embarrassment. Her lips were quite red and her mouth invitingly pursed up into a shape suggesting readiness for a kiss. This was not inviting, though, to Trakl. He simply regarded her in a theoretical sort of fashion as "attractive." Her manner of speaking he compared to the clucking of a chicken. In her English, everything had the same intonation. Because of this lack of, or mistaken, emphasis, no one learned anything at all from her about Egypt's past. How deep do her thoughts go on the subject of taking the veil, of becoming a more devout and traditional Muslim? Trakl was thinking this while the young woman guide Aneha was looking at him sideways and at all the rest of the group. They seemed to her no better than animals. She didn't like animals. These people lacked Egyptian good humor and other attractive qualities. I am longing not for my children and not for my Egyptian husband but so much simply to be walking by the sea. Anyway, away from this river, this fateful long river that goes through the sand. She wanted some rest. She did not want to wake up in bed with Trakl, and she never did. Life was not long enough for that.

STUCK

Downstairs the children were very busy on the machines, looms they were, they were six and seven and eight to ten years old, boys and girls, weaving; their results were placemats dresses and rugs. Mostly rugs. Their little fingers popped around the looms with considerable skill. Their faces and eyes were nervous as they turned around. The money was stuck to the pockets of the American crowd, as if velcroed to their thighs' clothed walls. To give was to condone the enterprise. This enterprise seemed in no way laudable. It was announced, very improbably, that doing this work, the children made money that would enable them to go to school. Abdullah Ragui was one of these children, nine years old. Across the river (the Nile—there weren't any others) small figures of men, women, and animals were performing tasks necessary for survival. None had—or could be seen to have—a skill like Abdullah Ragui's. Ptit ptit ptit ptat ptatt! her fingers raced across the loom. There were no answers to the questions the tourists had. Some bought rugs, to bridge the gap. That act left responsibility for being kind to the children to the men who sold the rugs. They would give the children money or they would not. Certainly, Doctor Petersen thought, if they gave it, they wouldn't share it but only give them a little bit. If I, though, give this child (Abdullah) a lot—he imagined a man taking it from her forcibly, hurting her little hand. He thought, We are stuck, and these children are stuck. Even the awful (probably) men who sell the rugs are stuck, and there is no good my trying to get out of it by not giving money to a child. He gave a few dollars to Abdullah. Thank you, she said, and went back feverishly, going faster than ever, to her task, as if such violent energy were what had brought the gift about.

LUXOR

I burst into tears when I saw the Temple of Luxor. My woman friend and I had been quarreling; throughout this brief but difficult trip we had a very hard time. We were to break up within a month. More precisely, she would leave me. I would alternately love her and detest her. I would fall down on the floor and cry. These would be hard cries. But now I was in Luxor, on a trip to Egypt, and I had no idea that any of this would happen. Then why did I cry? Why, when I looked the first time at those soaring columns, and then quickly looked again, as if to verify that the cause was there, did I burst, collapse, into bitter and almost uncontrollable tears? Something weighed down on me. Don't boss me around, she said. I had said, too many times, on the boat, Don't drink the water. As this kind of problem shows, I was too old for her. I was probably too old for her. Luxor, not too old for me, was electrifying in its presence. The temple was just old, and just repaired, enough. I certainly didn't identify myself with the temple. Nor was it like my friend, though in a way it reminded me of her legs. I admired the simultaneous shapeliness and solidity of those legs. Sometimes, she put one over me in the morning to help me to sleep when I would wake up too early. It made my anxiety go away. So did Luxor—by being so grand, so beautiful, and such a relief from the waste of the rest of that trip.

DEAD

Tet, Hathor, and Osiris were getting ready to welcome a newcomer to the Land of the Dead.

Big temple was there but it was useless. No one lived in it. It was still there for the purpose of what was left of the Dead.

After three thousand years can you feel sorry for the dead? You feel perhaps a little shiver, and that's that. But they have been dead for such a long time that you think, well, after all they are really genuinely dead. One doesn't have to worry about them so much.

Docrow stubbed his toe on an unseen step hidden by sand at the Temple of Osiris-Pik. Ouch ouch! he lay down bending his right ankle, the one with the painful toe, in his hand. Oooh, damn it!

He wasn't dead. One doesn't die from a stubbed toe. Maybe, though, a scorpion had bitten him.

He dreamed he was walking along a dusty white road with a bird-headed individual. He dreamed of being ferried across a river on a boat as he lay flat on his back and wrapped up in cloth. He dreamed of being welcomed by animal-headed people, being gestured to, being handed an ivory staff.

Hathor was dressed in blue silks to receive him. She had the shoulders and the body of a woman but the head of a cow. She was beautiful.

She was Marie-Christine, the woman he had seen on the tourist boat earlier in the day, crossing from the West (Land of the Dead) bank of the Nile to the East (Land of the Living).

The pilot of that boat was Tet. The man who went about taking people's tickets was Osiris.

He himself, Docrow, wore a wrinkled white shirt. It was barely presentable. Now, however, he was dressed in gold. He solemnly received the gods' greetings and never for the rest of time did anything else.

ON FOUR CONTINENTS
Six Stories

IN WEED

The shutters were open, so you could see out of the dance hall. There was mountain outside. Also the door was open. There was an almost chilly breeze.

The name of this place was Weed, California. That was actually its name, Weed.

She looked very beautiful. He looked wrinkled but fit. He was a soldier. She lived near there.

Of course, they never saw each other again.

Her hand held his as if each hand were a small animal, when they walked across the floor.

Goodnight!

LOSING

Of course! he thought, dissatisfied with Alice. I'd love to have this evening. I'd be much happier alone. And forever, too. Not just now. Eventually I'll find someone better for me than she is. In fact, once cut Alice loose from him and he is desolate, despairing, off the walls. No wallpaper, no net, no ring of fire can hold him. He must have Alice back. All modern technology (telephone, etc.) was at his service but he would never get her back. He had made his characteristic mistake. Alice was totally unaware of this kind of error. She put on her black coat and was crying, crying bitterly at being unloved. In her calm way, then, eventually, she found someone else. Let humanity beware!

PHOTOGRAPHERS NEAR THE RAIN FOREST

Snap! He took her picture standing in a doorway. Snap! near a car parked by the curb.

Snap beneath a plane tree. Snap snap two in the place where they stopped to have a drink.

I'd like one cappuccino, she said. And he said, Just a Brazilian coffee.

IN AFRICA

After the market the sunlight hit their faces as they gradually worked their way inside the shadowing garden doors of the hotel.

His foot was in the door-turn when she went in.

Can you spend the night?

What would we do all night?

Who built this hotel?

UNAWARE OF THE DROUGHT
(after some lines by Wallace Stevens)

During this great hot spell it's impossible to get coffee, it makes the café too hot. Cold drinks are almost impossible to find. People hoard beer, soda, bottled water. Only here and there, an old sailor, drunk and asleep in his boots, wakes up with a terrible thirst and takes it for granted.

Rossini woke from a deep slumber and began to play the piano. I've got it! he cried. Bravo! Bravo! The wheat withers in the fields. A baby is crying. Of what use to us, after the opera is over, is Rossini? They heard scraps of Rossini's music everywhere. Springtime had come into its own. Despite everything, the child cried a little less. At the Teatro San Carlo they had the impression, known to be false, that time had just begun.

TO THE RED CROSS

Sitting by the Willimantic River, his idea and hers, she shows him her Notebook which is full of "sayings," quotations Betty's copied down from poetry, about nature and even more about love. How corny it is, he thinks— how much I love her! He didn't exactly love her. High in the hills of Saipan, she let him take the jeep, he took her hand. Betty if we were— Yes, I know, she said, someplace else. He was an enlisted man and she of an order (the Red Cross) that was reserved, so far as socializing went, for officers. A mere private, such as he was, had no right to place his hand on her arm. She had a romantic sentimental however you want to call it maybe even melodramatic philosophizing attitude about life, which was one of the things that led her to join the Red Cross. He felt adventurous and ambitious at the same time. I have to leave tomorrow. Can you come to New York? I hope so—I don't know. The Red Cross was lucky to have had her for a few years, though the same could not be said of the army's having had him. She, two years older than he, was in a way of forever being a mother. A woman of twenty-four. Summer's coolness, her phrase book, and the light-reflecting trees!

OVER

Every day, near lunchtime, the small planes flew over and dropped explosives. No sooner had the men of the Third Platoon, Second Company, Third Regiment, of the Ninety-Sixth Infantry Division started opening their cans of food—carrotflake and beefcake—that was keeping them alive, than the zooming would be heard and soon, overhead, there were planes. Mouths anticipating eating, or already begun, the men dived into trenches. It was, luckily for the infantry, without fatality or even injury that these raids took place. One beautiful cloudless day, the planes didn't come. Not the next day, either, nor the day after that. After a while, the men got used to a quiet lunch. Then the company moved on; they had occupied this first position for fifteen days. Later, the planes came back to drop not bombs but pamphlets telling Americans to end the war. Like their other missions, this one was without result—in this case, the company wasn't there. Thirty years later, a man from this company and one of the pilots sat facing each other across a large oak table. They were drinking, looking around, and talking about electronic chips, as were the others at the table. Just as lunch began to be served, a violent noise came from the ceiling. On the floor above, someone, or something, had knocked over a pile of stacked-up chairs. "My God! A lunch-raid!" Hirschenson cried, and Kanamaka, astonished, knew what he meant.

SURRENDER

His heart beat furiously as he walked back and forth, trying to work out a scheme to keep his wife from going out. He wanted to keep her in the house.

He had been a colonel in the tank corps. He was frightening and stern. Orders from Supreme Command, his orderly said. He went to the military field phone. Mmmmmmm.

That was when Ivan surrendered his regiment. It snowed. He couldn't follow the order to go around and attack from the side because he knew that his entire regiment would be killed. He didn't surrender to save himself but to save his men. There was a principle. He felt he was right. Yet surrendering is always dubious, giving bad feelings because it gives you good feelings about those you hate. They put him to work in a factory in Germany and there he met her, his wife—she had been captured on the Russian front—and married her. After the war, they came to America. He was only twenty years older than she was, but sometimes it seemed like much more. He had some very old ideas about how a man and a woman should behave.

Ivan didn't learn English, he wanted things to be the same. Ekaterina had a dream that she was rescued from a blazing building and she walked forth from it into a field full of tall green grass and blue and red flowers. Ivan said, Mmmmhmmm; and she said, No not tonight. He would have surrendered, he thought, his regiment to her, again and again. But it was too late.

From the porch where he was walking back and forth,

he saw the bus. There was Ekaterina! His heart almost stopped, though he was a strong man. The bus stopped. He was running, but he couldn't reach it. The young woman, about twenty-nine, got in. Beautiful New Jersey spring day of yellows and lilacs, with stone-and-muddy streets. Hard breathing. He saw, as he reached the bus, which was leaving, and she gazed out the window, that it wasn't his wife at all, but a young American woman, who was shorter and had a slightly different chin.

AFTERWARDS

Did I ever really think of Ekaterina? he thought. Of her happiness in and for herself? Meeting again after thirteen years, they went to a baseball game. She had gained not much but a little weight, and her face no longer had quite that angle of beauty that had cut him like a knife. Never in his life had he been so happy, nor so bloody. He walked through New York like a wound. She had entered into his system (bones, nerves, blood vessels, arteries, brain) like a necessity, and death and time were the only necessities that could drive her out. He felt now a touch of that old electricity, a spring day after many cold nights, and he stared at the stone seatway beneath him and at the yellow railings above it and at the backs and the hair and the caps of the persons seated in front of him and thought he understood what it had all been about. "You may visit, like Turgenev, on our porch, and see her, or you can stop seeing her entirely," her husband said. "You may choose either of these ways. But you may not make love to my wife, or else you'll die." Fair enough!

Well, Lennie, he said. He felt awkward and cool. She felt, as she did often in these early days of her pregnancy, nauseated. She did not say, "I feel nauseous." Lennie had learned English as a child, learned it just about perfectly. Her native tongue was Yiddish.

Hobhouse was Jewish on his mother's side and half-Jewish on his father's. The non-Jewish half of his father's was where the name Hobhouse came from.

Hobhouse admired Lennie's intelligence and her petite qualities.

They were, however, in the midst of a crisis now. Lennie's parents were urgently pressing her to name the child Schnerdel if it was a boy, and Schnerdelin if it was a girl.

Hobhouse thought these names absurd and said so.

Then I won't have the baby, Lennie said.

What? said Hobhouse. He couldn't believe it. This was a totally exaggerated and ridiculous threat.

Don't you figure they'll be upset if you don't have the baby?

No, not really, Lennie said. Not having a baby may be disguised as a quirk of fate, but not giving it the name my parents want can hardly be masked as an accident.

If you don't have the baby, you'll never see me again.

It will be a boy, said Lennie, and it will be like you and I will have it and hold it and know that you are never gone from me entirely.

You mean if I leave you'd go ahead and have the son?

Yes, and I'll name it Schnerdel.

But I only said I'd leave if you didn't have the child!

I won't have it if I can't name it Schnerdel, she said.

Then, he said, you'll be alone.

When will you leave? she asked.

Well, obviously not until you make it impossible for the child to be born.

You're in as much of a hurry as that? she cried. To murder your son?

No, not that at all, he said, not knowing and by this time not really caring if he was winning or losing, I want you to *have* the child. Agh! Name it Schnerdel if you want to. But what a terrible name! How would you like to be sitting in a classroom and have the teacher call out your name Schnerdel.

Mine would be Schnerdelin, Lennie said.

Hobhouse thought he might be going crazy. But aren't you glad it's not? he said.

Listen, Lennie, he said. Isn't this *our* baby. Don't we have the right to name it what we want?

She said, I want to name it Schnerdel (or Schnerdelin).

Lennie, he said, don't you think you and I should *agree* on the name of our child?

Yes, of course I do, and I don't know why you won't, she said.

Lennie and Hobhouse were in the "Florida room" of their recently purchased home in Coral Gables. A child named Schnerdel or Schnerdelin in Coral Gables would have a severe handicap. Actually, almost any place English was spoken, but especially in the United States, Schnerdel or Schnerdelin would be a disadvantageous name. To help parents realize this, the Schnerdelin truck will go around. Each Coral Gables (and then other cities) neighborhood will be visited by a sound truck that blasts out various possible children's names: Kenneth, Anthony, Bruce, Edgar, Samuel, Emily, Ruth, Channukah, and Elizabeth, for example. Then the voice will say, Compare these relatively "normal" names to such a name as Schnerdel, or Schnerdelin. Why would any parent be so cruel as to give a child a name like that?

Lennie looked concerned. Hob was behaving oddly. What, what did you say? she said. She had heard him mumble something, but it didn't seem to be to her.

For a moment, he'd been asleep—oh!

I'm sorry, Hobhouse said. I guess I went to sleep. Listen, he said, Lennie, do what you want, but the truck was right—Schnerdel or Schnerdelin would be a mistake!

Wait! Lennie said. What truck?

I saw it, Hobhouse said, standing up. His white linen trousers, his white shoes, his white cotton shirt. He was wavering. Lennie felt concerned.

I guess, he said, Hobhouse is a funny name, too. Lennie is not so great, Lennie said. Maybe, though, Hobhouse said, we can do better for our child.

Oh you do want to have him! Lennie cried.

Of course I do, Hobhouse said. Otherwise I wouldn't be concerned with what we name him. Or her. Listen, at last he had a compromise idea, could we stop this quarrel and agree and compromise on one thing?

On what? Lennie said.

Sneddle, Hobhouse said—he was starting to drift off into a dream again, he could feel it, it made him a little afraid. Lennie, I have to get some rest.

We'll talk about it tomorrow, Lennie said.

No, Hobhouse said. Or well yes all right. But about this one thing I'm clear. Sneddle. How would that be as a compromise? You can pronounce it however you want when your parents are around.

And for the girl? Lennie said.

Sneddelin, said Hob.

Do you really think that's better? Lennie asked. Sneddle, Schnerdel, what's the difference?

There's a difference to me, Hobhouse said. He felt his lack of complete Jewishness was making him clear—or unclear.

Lennie was smiling. Of course we can give it (girl or boy) a middle name too—maybe even (she hesitated as if she might be violating a sacrament) even John, or Jane. He reached out his arms to her but she was against him before that. Oh Hobhouse, I thought we were really going to lose it! What? he exclaimed. "Sneddle John Weismuller," she said.

LIVING IN THE SUN

Terence was a painter. He said he wanted to be a black iris—whatever that meant. By sunset he was often drunk. He threw a glass of beer at me, that's how I met him. He was sitting in the Aga Rheion Café with a beer beside him, and drawing. He said he threw it because I looked pretentious. He also must have known I wouldn't retaliate, and that if I had, he could have gone into an act, of being drunken, helpless, insane. I was, on the contrary, interested and pleased that a beer was heading for me: I felt lonely. My wife and daughter were there, but we had, up till that moment, made no connection with anyone else. This drunkenness of Terence (to which I owed our friendship), if it started in the afternoon, usually lasted till ten or eleven, when those who can stand the thought of getting into it are beginning to think of bed. At this time of night Terence slightly perked up. He talked and talked, sometimes at his very best, making it harder for anyone to leave him—which may have been an unconscious (?) purpose of his being, at this hour, so entertaining, so loquacious. For those who knew him and liked him, Terence's drunkenness was as essential a part of life there as the sea, the tar, the broken glass, the tiny white chapel built to the Virgin by a sailor, the cliffs, the dry fig trees, the idea of going to Mandraki to drink ouzo and eat fish. "Let's Rilk," Terence said. That's fine with me. To "Rilk" was to respond in an exaggeratedly oversensitive way, as Terence believed Rilke did, to everything. Oh the unerring orchidism of the waves! Terence cried. Oh, help, hic! Terence said. I'm Rilking again! He also had considerable disdain for the French. Oh, vraiment, Terence said. Quel snobisme per-pét-u-el! Tant pis! he groaned. And Je suis désolé. The French language he considered an affront and everyone who spoke it was a fink. Bloo-ulp! Terence said. Let me introduce you to Margaret. She is a real black iris, aren't you Margaret? Ah, what? Margaret said. She was a nice young woman. When Terence was sober (I more often saw him this way years later, in New York, before he died), he was a little bit dry and wistful, brittle almost, like paper that has gotten wet and then was very vigorously dried out by too much heat. Underneath this dry plainness, though, Terence was crazy. With alcohol he was able to leap over the dry phase into the exalted, funny one. The island, Hydra, was sort of a hospital, at least for a while. Life there was relatively undangerous and had simple, regular lines. Finally, though, it simply didn't have the necessary equipment. Booze, boys, friends, octo-bits, Monsieur Oui-Oui's Restaurant, the non-electricity, the art school on the cliff, the non-doctors, the water shortage, Leonard, Arnold, the woman who came down to the harbor after seventy years, these weren't enough. Terence went back to New York. He was in the hospital and he painted. After six months he left, but they still have some of his paintings hanging up there. Apparently, by law, they belong to the hospital. When Terence was young, in his twenties, he was, I had heard, very beautiful. You could see it in him still, his beauty, and it was probably one of the reasons that certain people (the ones I knew about were women) became so unswervingly attached to him. He was very talented, too, and very smart. All of this he was always giving—if not throwing—away. In the heat of Hydra, in July, the sun was like a mallet and there was no way to work between lunch and the cool of late after-noon. Terence, though, sitting at a table in front of Mon-sieur Oui-Oui's, is working, with ink and pastels. A Pierrot head and a broad neck lead down to a rectangle in which are the names of three Ohio towns: Toledo, Akron, and Dayton. To the left of and somewhat below this, little pastel-colored balls (of chalk and smoke) emerge from the top of a head with a smudged green face. And to the right an ink-and-white ballerina points one toe down to his printed (I arrive just in time to see him sign it, or maybe he signs it because now I'm there) name, TERENCE.

SONGS OF THE AEGEAN

Black is the cover of my true love's hair. Stoffard sang as
he went out in the boat. The black was a yarmulke.
Stoffard was a comedian. This was his idea of a joke, a
Jewish version of an English folk song. For him his warm
wit blotted out all his troubles and even the sky. It was in
Greece—it may have been only the deep imagined com-
plications of the Greek past that made the simple silly
joke have a purity and a clarity that it couldn't have had
any place else. A big ship went by, far enough away not
to be a danger. A dog was curled up on the shore. Helen
smiled but didn't laugh as Stoffard sang the song. She
had heard it just an hour before, when Stoffard invented
it. Black is the cover. The salt water leaped up as Helen
looked over. And Stoffard was standing up, she's afraid
it may turn over, and he is singing a song. He places his
one hand on the boat's side nervously, feeling a little
splinter stick and says, God this is a terrific day. Helen,
Helen, don't you like it. Smile! Tell me you do! Helen
smiled as the sun hit her face. Now he is rowing, and the
boat leaps away. "Black is the cover." "And so we'll go no
more a-roving" had been sung there before. And "Kale
Khios," by the Greek sailors. And, long before that,
"Kore" and "Rododaktolos Eos—O Oinops Pontos."

CHRISTINE AND THE DOCTOR

Christine was fifteen going on sixteen, and, distressed that she had a little wart on her hand, she had a tendency to keep it out of handclasps with those to whom she was attracted. Her mother had married a second time; her stepfather was Robert Lindt, of San Clemente, California. Her mother, now Mrs. Lindt, was the former Barbara McLennon. Christine had brownish-blonde hair, which she wore long, and an alluring sideways look of her eyes. Dr. Motson asked Christine where she was going, and she said, "Over there." Over there was a place where you could hear the drums. Christine is walking along happily, when suddenly in her path there is a snake. A snake can go anywhere it wants. It is like a whole chess set in itself. It can go sideways, forward, backward, curving, and up; it can spiral, it can slip down like a sleeve; and it can strike like a hand-grenade and a clock. Christine was frightened. She ran back the white dusty road to the café where the doctor was drinking a cup of tea. What, Christine, what's wrong? said Dr. Motson. Oh well, there's a snake that's after me, Christine said. Motson went out on the road, leaving his teacup in its saucer on the tabletop beside which Christine stood, and looked around. He looked up then down the road. Down it he saw a smallish disappearing splat! as if a wire being pulled by an electrical contractor. Put that circuit over there! It was the snake. The snake was now going somewhere else. It did not, or perhaps could not, distinguish Christine from anyone else, although there was a chance that it knew she was a human. Motson came back to find Christine had sat down. She was smoking a cigarette. The doctor wiped off his brow. Do your parents allow you to do that? he asked. He said, I did see the snake and he's gone. No, Christine said; and Well thank you I was scared, but now I think I'm going to walk a different way. That night in the restaurant Christine told her parents that she had seen Dr. Motson. Dr. Motson? Where were you walking that you saw him? her stepfather said. Oh, out that way, said Christine, pointing, she didn't know the names of the streets in this town. He saved me from a snake. Her mother also still had rather long hair. She had a shrimp on a fork, and a white silk blouse. Tell us the story, she said.

AFTER THE ELISIR

Complimenti, the tall good-looking young man said.
Maestro, complimenti. Thanks, grazie, answered the
maestro. Followed a brief conversation in Italian. The
young man turned to his friend. Est-ce que vous parlez
italien? No, only English and français said the lumplike
but equally tall young man in a black suit standing there
also. He says (the maestro, that is) you look Italian. I
take that as a great compliment, the lumplike young man
said. He was making lots of money. The tall, good-looking one seems a little weak, something of a toady. Meanwhile, quickly, the two tall young men had gone. My
daughter Graziana and I were alone with the maestro.
This was the moment that no one had been waiting for.
The maestro's mother just before had been whisked off
to see the Star, in his dressing room above. The maestro
was permanently married. When we went out into the
corridor, Graziana, I noticed, was looking, but aside
from a long radiator, there was nothing much to see. She
is puzzled by opera. She doesn't know exactly what its
great appeal for her is. But it is certainly appealing; it is
sometimes overwhelming, like a fireworks display in the
heart. Directing it, the maestro said, was *divertente,* full
of adventures. The Star, who is over fifty, has considerable fear of losing his voice. The maestro's mother is
eighty-two. She has a somewhat frail presence but a very
commanding voice, especially on the telephone. The
maestro is unable to prevent her from following him to
his performances all over the world. The Lump and the
Goodlook (Toady) have the American rights to the

work. Many of the artists, including the Star, whom the maestro's mother had just gone up to meet, are under long-time contract to their firm.

THE INTERPRETATION OF DREAMS

The small bird's wings on the bare tree had in the uneven sunlight the look of wood chips. This brought back a memory. He was standing in a park. In his hand he held a long thin bean. Inside it there were kernel-like or pea-like things encased in goo and stickiness. He knew they were not meant to eat. He had a dream about this park, in which he found the beans, that reminded him of Marina. She had been gone for twenty years. In the dream she was someone else. She was also a boy, named Keekle. He ran to his house, it was really a collection of little houses around a court but the buildings were connected. He ran very very fast. I'm lost, he thought. The collie was big and fluffy. The dog's name was Stizzy, pronounced Stitzy. His hair was always coming off on the furniture. He found time to look at the collie but Marina did not. Proposed they go to the opera or the theatre. Our life is dramatic enough, said Marina. I don't see how it could be any more dramatic than it is. Who needs the theatre? In Paris the snow is falling outside his rue de Fleurus hotel. He has never seen Marina, and won't for another four years. The apartment is dark and there is snow out. A friend calls him on the phone. When will we see you? Life is going by so fast. Stizzy has not come home. He phoned Marina. The operator said there was no such number. Marina, he thought, is crossing her slim legs now in Boston or in Los Angeles or wherever she has gone to live. Her thin dress. The earrings I bought for her at the fruit store that spread out its goods on the sidewalk. Wearing a nightgown, she came to his bedside and said, "Why?" There were long corridors open and latticed to the night air. There were dredgings, upheavals, transportings, roarings of the sea. Curtains flew. He was unable to answer, because he didn't know why. Why things had to be the way they were. Why his life with Marina remained only a possibility, a set, or a foreground. Why he had never imagined it as anything else. Why? Why? Marina (the dream image of Marina) said. Keekle ran in and Marina wasn't there any more. He knew a foolish mistake was thinking that Keekle was as important as Marina, that his dreams were as important as what really happened. What knowing Marina excited in him, most deeply of all, was his childhood. A new wave of freshness, of absolute springtime, broke over his eyelashes like hail. He stood in the park with the bean. It was reddish black and had more or less the shape of a wisteria seedpod. It had an acrid smell. He knew that there were certain things in nature that you were never supposed to eat, even to raise to your lips. Tucking it under its wing, his love relationship with Marina had soared off, like the swan that it wasn't, with his childhood as it was only once, or maybe five thousand times, he could no longer tell, since it was really gone.

THE LAW

Are we allowed to do this? he said.

She was tied up almost in a knot on their bed.

She was smiling. No, she said. I don't think so.

He said, Why are we allowed to do this? Why isn't it against the law?

He spoke about the law as if he expected someone, or some force, to be vigilant at all times, at every second of his life.

If he was looking for this, the Conscience was available, or its more dreaded unreasonable compatriot, the Superego.

Of course he enjoyed the lawlessness, the violence and the humorousness of what he was doing.

Her wrists were tied to her ankles. That was enough.

She sighed. She moaned. She said Oh! Oh! She laughed, I think it is against the law.

How could people be allowed to have so much pleasure in such a funny way?

Vavoom! She had a pleasure that almost knocked him down.

He started to untie the ropes but she: "Let's do that again!"

He said. All right. Then, Just a minute.

He walked to the wall and looked out the window at the car. It was green in the chalky October light.

"All right," he said. And she: Ymm. Hummmm.

This second time it was slower, and sweeter than, and not so violent as, the first.

Afterward, she stood up, stretched, leaning her back against the wall. "My goodness!"

IN BETWEEN

About every other day, it was an impulse she found it hard to resist, she called him up. As soon as she heard his voice answer, hello high or hello low or hello medium or sometimes a somewhat joke fake theatrical or accent hello, she hung up. She wanted to be sure he was all right and she felt that the sound of his voice could give her this information. She had left him while he was ill, she felt she had to, but her guilty feelings seemed unending. These feelings, in extreme and then more modified form, would last for years. When someone dies, there are similar feelings, and in these feelings, of guilty grief, there is no one to call. Instead, a person prays, speaks to the lost one in imagination, weeps and suddenly stops (this in some ways is like the hang-up call), may even write something down. But how can the person hope that the one who is gone will read it? Brrrr-ring! It is she again, he said. Wishing. For him, this communication, that was also noncommunication, was nourishing. Actually, he didn't know if it was she or not. He couldn't, as he sat, this time silently, with the instrument in his hand, hear even a breath.

THE BABY

I can't tell you any more than that. I'm going to have a baby.

Who is the father?

Well—I don't want to say. I don't think you'd get a fair idea of him from what I could say.

What does he do?

Nothing, now. I don't want to say.

Do you like all this? Do you love him?

Yes. I like having a baby. I'm very excited . . . I dreamed about it last night .

I *dreamed* about it. It talked to me, even though it was just a baby (she says *bay*-bee). It was a little girl. And she talked to me. She said something funny and made me laugh.

What did she say? Do you remember?

No. I'm trying. I wish I could.I *loved* it. Listen, I have to go. This person is here, the father, I mean, and I can't really talk now.

Write me. Please?

Six years ago she said to him, Oh, something is terrible. He asked what. She said, I have to tell you. What. I'm pregnant. Oh, he said. He was elated. He thought there had been something wrong. He'd been afraid she would go back to someone else. That's wonderful! he said. What? she said. He said, Wonderful. I love you. Do you want to have the baby and get married? What? she said. No, I can't. Listen, but I love you, too.

Six years went by, with separations, reunions, and finally some fear and some indifference—not indifference but forgetting.

This second conversation (it was between two cities) was both unbearable and bearable. Now they are both waiting for the baby to be born.

THE DRUMMER:
A OAXACA LEGEND

The Corpse was walking slowly through the fields of central Mexico. This Corpse wore a gray hat, had a black dot-dot-dot-dot smile, black dot eyes, and cotton stuck against its head sides for hair. As it walked, it was swinging its arms. It also kept turning its head. The Corpse was looking for something, that was pretty sure.

The Corpse had been walking for almost three hundred miles, from Mexico City to where it was now, this side of Oaxaca. Its walk had taken it ten and a half days. Some people say Corpses walk fast, and some say they walk slow. One thing this Corpse did, whether fast or slow, was to keep walking. It didn't slow down through towns or go to sleep at night.

The Corpse was headed for the town of Oaxaca. It had a sister who was there, who was still alive. And it wanted her to do something for it. Him, I suppose we might as well call it, since from the build of it, it seemed to be a man.

When the Corpse found his sister, she was at first very scared but then when she calmed down she agreed to do what it said. He asked her to go to the Church of the Soledad, which had a whole little part of the town that was built up into and around it, and ask the Bishop there (the priest there was a bishop) for a set of drums that the Corpse used to play on when he was a boy and he was alive, before he'd left Oaxaca to go to the center. Now, once dead, he wanted to play the drums again and he thought he would like to play those.

His sister went there and asked. Those drums had been broken for some years. The priest said, though, that he had a boy there, whom he would tell to make the Corpse a new but similar set of drums.

The boy, Paco, worked on the drums, and the days sped past. When the drums were finally ready, not the sister but the Corpse himself came to get them. It was just before the time of a service, and when the people saw him, they fainted away. The Corpse took up the drums and placed them on the altar, beside the place where the Bishop usually stood. Then the Corpse played, putting into the music all he had learned of what it was like to be dead. It made extraordinary music, and the people woke up and felt happy. The Bishop came up to the altar and stood beside the Corpse. On its other side, the people all at once noticed, there was a beautiful young woman, in white, attired and also winged like an angel, and who was also a bride. It was the Corpse's dead girlfriend, Ramona, whom he had left behind when he went to Mexico City to work in a plant.

The people listening to the amazing music realized that it was a privileged moment. When it ended, chances were, the Corpse and Ramona would return to the world of death. Even while the Corpse still drummed—it did so for ten hours—people began to beg the Bishop to find some way to save the Corpses. The Bishop himself had been hoping for the same thing, praying that it be the Lord's will. Upon being thought about so intensely, the Lord snapped into action and looked down at Oaxaca. The Lord was, after millennia of isolation, only in the vaguest way sensitive to earthly music. But he saw that the people listening to the Corpse were happy. So he said, Yes, the Corpse—and I guess along with him Ramona—may return to life for seven years, if he so wishes. After which time I would like him to come up into heaven, to play the drums for me. It's a long time that I've been without the blessing of that kind of sound. Thank you, Lord, the Bishop said. And then, daring, But Lord, be patient. What are years to you? Let this man live twenty-eight years and the woman with him. Then take him to your breast. To my bandstand, the Lord said. Then, Yes, all right. Twenty-eight years it shall be. Whereat the Bishop turned to offer the Corpse life. But the Corpse was no longer there. A serious-faced young man of thirty-two was holding a pair of batons as if he didn't know where he was or what he was doing. A woman of twenty-nine stood nervously at his side. Well, what? Play, the Bishop said. You have been granted life. I guess I've played enough, the former Corpse said. He embraced Ramona, and came down. The great stamina of the dead was no longer his. He grew old peacefully in Oaxaca, as did Ramona. And when twenty-eight years were up, the Lord did not take him—he was living still. Indeed the Bishop had calculated that within twenty-eight years the Lord might forget his interest in hearing Mexican drums.

The Corpse then, when by ordinary standards he was over sixty, was living beyond his appointed time. However, in the sixty years that were counted as his normal span, four of those had been spent dead. Thus there were four years that were still due him, which the Lord, being the Lord, did not forget. So that, when he was sixty-four, Javier happily died, and Ramona died with him, and at the graveyard, they being poor, there was no tombstone, but the Lord at the last minute sent one down that was in the shape of a large drum.

This story is still told in the streets and in the bodegas of Oaxaca and in the surrounding towns. In Acuitlán the Corpse is changed to the corpse of a lion, which performs acrobatic feats. And in Cuzuno, it is the corpse only of a huge pair of feet, which dance. Ramona does not figure in these two versions, but in others she is the more prominent figure. In the tiny village of Suninos, Ramona is the traveling Corpse; she comes to the almost-larger-than-the-village church of Suninos, mounts the altar, and sings. No one has ever heard such songs. The Lord is so moved by her singing that he thinks of reviving the heavenly angelic choir. Her lover, Javier, appears in this version as a minor character, as Ramona does in the first.

A MIRACLE OF SAINT BRASOS

The number of Corpses living in Oaxaca was growing. When it reached three hundred, a meeting of the Town Council was called. Something had to be done. So great a number of Corpses might change life in the town for the worse. Jobs and living space were limited. The Corpses might deprive people of both. In fact (it was persuasively argued by a prominent citizen who lived with one of the Corpses, his brother, and knew their ways) there was nothing to fear. As far as jobs went, the Corpses did kinds of work that were all their own and were in no competition with the Living. As for lodging, Corpses who didn't stay with relatives lived in ramshackle places outside town that they had built on otherwise unvalued property. Nor did the living dead encroach on Oaxaca's supply of food—they ate special dishes, composed of leftovers; and in fact one of the Corpses' main activities was gathering leftover food and repreparing it in special "Corpse" restaurants, to which other Corpses flocked every day—to Las Momias, Su Muerte, and El Skeletòn. Other Corpse occupations were playing drums, sifting through heaps of rubble, and repairing lost, wrecked, and abandoned cars. In these cars, the Corpses sometimes drove, on Sunday afternoons, in the surrounding country, large numbers of them—eight or nine—in each car; they drove slowly, said little, and looked around, grateful for their presence in the midst of life.

The Town Council meeting ended in a spirit of good feeling, but the Corpses were nervous all the same and soon after called a meeting of their own. They wished to find a way to contribute something useful to Oaxacan life. A Corpse Used-Car Lot was proposed, at which the cars that they put back together would be sold, at cost, to the Living. In this way the citizens of Oaxaca would have an almost endless supply of inexpensive used cars, and good ones at that—the Corpses were expert mechanics. We run the risk of seeming useless, said one Corpse, Alonso Betraens; there are so many useful things that we cannot do. Corpses couldn't plant or harvest crops, couldn't serve as guides to the nearby ruins, couldn't practice medicine (who would go to a dead person to be protected from death?) or law—the dead, though not exempt from the law, were regarded as in some way outside it. We can certainly make cars, though, he said (and here all applauded); and driving in them, Oaxacans will be grateful and will sense our utility to their lives. I think it is a great proposal. The proposal was approved.

The car-sale facility was quickly set up. The Living thronged to the lot, and it seemed the Corpses couldn't make cars fast enough to satisfy the needs of Oaxacans. Esteem for the Corpses grew, and there began to be a kind of sunny happiness in their lives that had not been there before. Only a little—they were still very much second-class citizens—but something positive, nonetheless.

In April, about four months after the car sales began, the criminal saint, Brasos de Guadalajara, was in Oaxaca. He bought from the Corpses a high-roofed white De Soto from a very long time past, which had room for his robes and his halo, and spent a part of every day driving it around. Every day he did so, every day he stayed in Oaxaca, there were two or three more persons dead. It seemed evident to the people of Oaxaca that this strange Being in a corpse-car was related to, and probably the cause of, all these deaths. It should be said that Brasos's robes and halo were invisible to mortal eyes. Feeling began to turn against the Corpses. This murderer, in one of their cars, was one with them. Wasn't it most likely that he had been brought there to kill the Living and to thereby increase the number of Corpses and bring them closer to being a majority in Oaxaca? The "Cemetery Springtime" mood the selling of the cars had brought at first was now at an end, replaced by suspicion and fear, even hatred. Seated in the De los Muertos Mole Restaurant, four eminent Corpses of Oaxaca convened, urgently, to seek a solution to the problems that the man in the De Soto had caused. Reluctantly, they determined that they would have to kill him. His actions seemed not only destructive but also incomprehensible, without reason. In fact, he was there to carry out a revenge on twenty prominent Oaxacans who had behaved fraudulently in the reconstruction of Santa Maria de la Soledad, the great church that was the dearest to Saint Brasos in all Mexico. It was here he had been baptized, and here he had, at only two months old, first attempted (and miraculously, successfully!) to climb up the great stone cross on the central altar and to sing to the assembled citizens. His family moved to Guadalajara but Brasos did not forget the Soledad. Every year he had made a pilgrimage to it. Usually it was only for a day, but this time it was for longer, for as long as it took to eliminate those who had cheated on materials and labor, so that, if nothing were done, in ten or fifteen years the great sad church would collapse. Now, by the morning of the de los Muertos Mole meeting, Brasos had killed the first nineteen. The last, Homeró Gómez, Brasos did not kill immediately, but with his Saint-sense informing him that something was wrong, he instead bound him and placed him in his car, which he drove to the building of the Town Council. The four eminent Corpses, having come out of the hill-top restaurant, which was located just above the Council building, recognized the De Soto and immediately bringing automatic weapons to their shoulders began to fire on the man who came out of it. They fired two hundred rounds. The man they destroyed was not whom they suspected, but Homeró Gómez. Saint Brasos had sent him out as a decoy. With the twenty malefactors now dead, the saint was ready to enact the last part of his plan: to explain his actions to the Town Council, and to give them the money to rebuild the church. The Council were frightened, but they were convinced. By a powerful act of his will, Saint Brasos enabled them to see his halo and his robes. He gave them the money he had taken from those guilty of fraud: it was thirty-five billion pesos. Leaving the room, he once turned back. Mind you spend every peso on the church, Saint Brasos said. And mind you build it well. If you do not, I guarantee you (here he let them see his halo again) that every single one of you, and everyone else in this town, except for the women and children, will be most definitively dead. Then he left, the mission he had set for himself being accomplished. The members of the Council, believing that Brasos, along with whatever else he might be, was also an emissary of, and perhaps even a King or Divinity of the Dead, re-solved not only to repair the great church but also to do everything possible to improve the status of Corpses. This meant granting them rights they hadn't had: the right to own property, and to attend school; Corpses could serve as guides to archeological sites, and if they were qualified, could even practice law. So life improved for the living dead in ways they could not have dreamed of when they made their modest decision to sell used cars. Brasos, who had himself been dead for hundreds of years, did not plan this change, though it was his miraculous behavior that brought it about.

A MAN OF THE CLOTH

"It's odd to be dead and making cars."

"It's kind of a confusion!"

"Explain it to me."

Mrs. Wallabee is standing talking to the Corpses working in the used-car yard. "Why don't you people just enjoy your life, er, uh, death?" she stumblingly said.

"We like to make a contribution," an old Corpse said.

"It's a job," said a younger one.

"'Tis fun," said another. And then one other, "It is good to be occupied, Señora. To do the Lord's work."

This last one who spoke was a dead priest.

He still bore the uniform: high collar, etc.

"Why don't you do priest's work 'mong the dead?" quavered Miss Halberstrom, Mrs. Wallabee's "companion." Were these two lovers? the priest wondered, but it was, he knew, none of his business.

So far from him they were, norteamericanas, gringas—and the living as well. True, some day they might be dead, even among the living dead. But they would probably not be down there, down here, in Mexico.

He felt a stab of lust for Miss Halberstrom. But that, too, was inappropriate. What beautiful young woman would want a dead lover? and a priest, or ex-priest, at that?

"Well, Miss Halberstrom," he began. How did you know my name? she said. "The dead know everything." He laughed. "I saw it on your button," he said. In fact, Miss Halberstrom was wearing a large off-white plastic button that said HALBERSTROM, MISS on it. It was a badge given her to permit her entry into a soft-drink plant outside Oaxaca.

This priest was an interesting man. He was dead but seemed more full of life than anyone she had ever met.

Violet Halberstrom did not have lesbian longings and was not the companion in that sense of Mrs. Wallabee. They were merely *compagnons de route*. They had met when Mrs. Wallabee's car broke down in Albuquerque and had decided to drive down here together.

The ex-priest had scored a kind of hit with Miss Violet Halberstrom. Her live eyes exchanged with his dead ones some incantatory gleams.

"I could settle down here," she thought. "And work for the dead. I think that I could love this priest."

The summer was very hot. Father Jimenez said, "The reason I do not do priest's work is that my fellows here, the dead, have no need for it. Above all, that work is to prepare people for death."

How interesting! Mrs. Wallabee had grown silent. She sensed that there was something going on between her traveling companion and the dead priest. She, too, lusted for Violet Halberstrom, although Violet did not know it. The priest's suspicion had been based on something real.

It was difficult not to desire Violet Halberstrom. This young woman was truly a beautiful ripe peach, nectarine, whatever.

Time buzzed around her. One wanted to join in with time.

"Violet! Tell me that you care for me!"

"Of course I care for you! But I also care for other things."

That is what is so attractive about you, the priest thought.

Then he seemed of a sudden to remember what he was supposed to be doing.

"Are you ladies interested in a car? We can make you different kinds, either one based on one model or combining several. Take a look around."

Miss Halberstrom, looking, wandered, and the priest gazed at her. It had been like this, he remembered, too, when he was alive and had taken death on him, to become a priest.

IN CHINA

He got in his car and asked the chauffeur to drive him to the office where he was going to work that day. It was very early in the morning but already there were thousands of people in the streets. Almost all of them were riding bicycles. As the morning grew warmer and the pink sun lifted itself above the silvery coverlets of the clouds, the streets were even more filled with working-day life. Hurry, the official said. Hurry! But the chauffeur could not hurry because of the immense crowds in the streets. Tomorrow we will start earlier, the official said. Meanwhile, please, go quickly. Do the very best you can. The magician, who was waiting for the arrival of this official who was scheduled to rehire him for another six-month stint on the Huangpu River Cruise boat, lackadaisically did a few tricks—palming objects, taking things out of his sleeves, cutting and then restoring to its wholeness a length of rope. The official meanwhile was working with a little computer, which kept catching brighter and brighter yellow rays of the early morning sun. According to what I've calculated, he thought, it will be simpler to give him a contract for the whole year. That will lessen my responsibilities and will also spare him the unpleasant suspense of waiting once again to see if his work is approved. His work seems to me very satisfactory. And there is no reason to suspect that a magician of his calibre and of his rank will suddenly become an unreliable or unpatriotic performer. So let it be! Xu Zhang won't object. I'll have the final permission later today. This work and these thoughts done, the car has arrived and here is the magician, he sees him, entering his office. By now the sun is quite bright yellow white. Ah, Bo Hong, the official says, this morning I have good news for you. I really do!

MAN WOMAN AND DOG

The dog stayed in the car. She went into the café. Auguste was sitting at a little round table right next to the big glass movable walls through which you could see what was happening on the street. Althea felt a discomfort in the front seat so she jumped into the back. He turned around and started then continued to get up to help her sit down in her chair. On light front feet, for a moment, the dog bounced. She had a bouncy sensation. Once she had her body collected in the back, she turned, rearranged herself and sat down, or rather, sat up. Her nose now was lightly touching the window. Her slender legs ran down from her throat to the seat. Hello, doggie! a passerby noted. What will you have, he ordered. She stayed coffee. Two bills, all right. The waiter crescendoed, beckoned. A five-o'clock laugh. It's quite early. She rearranged themselves. We spoke. We went to bed too early, she said. Made love. At first he didn't argue with her theory. The dog was not accustomed to being in Paris at this hour. Usually it was later or earlier. There was something in the light that made her keep turning her head about. He said, If we hadn't made love too soon we probably wouldn't have made love at all. A big dark man was walking determinedly down the street. I think this man must have resembled a man who once accidentally kicked her. When he passed, she whined. He looked, she whined. He smiled hand-gesture, she kept whining. Eh, chien, he said and he walked along. Jean-Christophe said: Why are women always ecstatic when they make love, whereas for us men such ecstasy is fairly rare? The woman, Robert said, because the woman is always in love when she makes love. Otherwise she doesn't do it. Well, possibly. Althea barked and barked and barked. Who was there to save her? The car's windows were closed. Ruhwahff, ruhruhrrwahwahfff, Althea cried. Hélène couldn't hear her, however. She had gone to the restroom to calm herself because she was crying. To readjust her face, too. When she came back upstairs Auguste was holding Althea, panting, hairily, on his lap. Who leaped at Hélène but Auguste didn't wholly let her go. Stop stay stop, he said. Althea'd been so upset in the car. She found it also rather nervous-making here. She smelled, so hot. A clean dog but an excited one. Hardly hold you on my lap. We can make love again, he said, around the neck of the dog. And this time may be just on time. This was clever but didn't approach the real subject: Are men, or men and women, incapable of love? And, beneath that: what. Mild anxiety moved the waiter the people in the street and the sunny haze. It filled them. It was the tone of the day, shared by Althea. Are you feeling better? he said. Yes. Maybe we should give her something to drink.

GENF

The working class Italian man unbundled an Italian loaf of bread with a large hollow in it filled with some kind of pungent meat. I have to get off at Geneva because, while talking flirtatiously to Sandra, I neglected to go back to my compartment when the train crossed the border, and my bags, as a result, are in Austria. The Swiss promise to get them back to me sometime tomorrow. Sandra is a dancer and she has been dancing in Trieste. Now she lives in Geneva. She bends over slightly in the corridor. It attracts my attention. Her breasts are rather large and pretty, and this fact, at the thought of speaking to her, fills my body with a sort of heat—I find it a little too much actually—like steam heat in a hotel between seasons when, legally, it must be on but the weather doesn't necessitate it. Sandra, well, I say after I have found out, I have to get off the train. Can I see you tonight? Yes, she says, but remember you can't expect too much of me. I am involved with someone else. Involved—did Sandra say *involved* or did she say *engaged?* She didn't say *married.* Out on the lake in a boat the next late morning: Sandra, should I stay? In fact, may I stay? No, she says, nicely, and the wind blows. The Swiss find my bags. You've found them, so fast! I said. (The end of romance!) Yes, said the brisk fat fellow at the railroad counter—he is pleased—Dot's Svitzerland!

PETER AND CASSANDRA

Ronsard and his friend and fellow poet Valdeluzes were walking in the valley of the Var. Each was eighteen years old. Pierre had not yet laid eyes on Cassandre (Salviati), of whom his idealizations were to form the substance of his great collection, *Amours.* Marc (Valdeluzes) was somewhat in advance of Ronsard in this respect: he had already seen the girl about whom he was to write his best poems. Her name was Anne Desmoulins and she was the daughter of a lawyer in Boule-sur-Var. Ronsard was envious of his young friend's precocity in love. What will my love be like? Ronsard wondered. Ronsard knew he was a better poet than Valdeluzes, and in the field of poetry being worse or better was just about all that counted. What you actually wrote, how much, and on what subjects, were substantially less important than how good you were. In regard to his status in this department Ronsard felt quite at ease. Still, his life wasn't helping. And he did need some help. Perhaps, after all, he wasn't meant to be a great poet—where was his subject? In such a state of dreariness of mind, Ronsard reached, with his friend, the line of plane trees that signaled the southernmost extremity of the town of Blois. There, two years later, Ronsard met Cassandre Salviati for the first and only time. To her, and to his memory of their brief meeting, he wrote a startling number of sonnets in the succeeding years.

Cassandre Salviati is there, in her gray-white silks, her rosy cheek, her ivory hand, a fan, green, in her left hand, oh she is dancing. Ronsard, clutch your heart! You can't reach it. No way to get to it. Your blood is beating. Something is. A violence, deep inside, caused by the outside. What a miracle! Quickly, go home and write!

Years later, shaken, distressed, Ronsard signed off writing about love in the following sonnet:

> That Love which tried to place me in the tomb,
> With weeping trees around Himself now lies
> In so dark place not even that Her Eyes
> Can enter there nor her Fair Limbs find room.
> Love that did lead me on and promised Soon
> Shall you find haven surer than the skies'
> Then left me piercèd and away He flies
> Now is Himself as dead in Time's cocoon.
>
> Midway to love and death I turned aside
> Said I shall love no more, no more compose
> Poems to what in death may solely end.
> Whereupon Love grew suddenly my friend,
> Implored me, begged me, promised her as bride,
> But I affixed a funerary rose.[1]

[1] *Ce dieu qu'au tombeau me mettre tentait* (Sonnet M)

UNKNOWN

The desire came back to him, but the girl was gone. Girl! She was a woman now, and had been for years. She had married six years after he'd met her, and that was in nineteen seventy-three. Now it was nineteen eight-six. She was fifteen (was that right?) when he saw her for the first time in her sister's house; her room was next to his. That means she is twenty-eight now. That is not very old! He, on the other hand, is nearly sixty. That is not very young! She thought of him with pleasure, too, but not with desire. For her his identity had been subsumed into the drama of her own life, of her being alive and fifteen. In an ancient culture they might have been monarchs together, she continuing on the throne after his death. She would weep for him, but he was gone. In her floods, her actual torrents and storms of tears, she would imagine he was back, and he would be, in a way, given watery body by what she felt. Now if he dies she probably won't know it. Her laundry is hung on the line. It's an old-fashioned way to do it but that is what she likes—clothes dried inside aren't the same. He imagines her with the three children, the husband, their quarrels, their making up. He sees this: in bed with Bernard, her husband, she turns over on one side, away from him, and with her right shoulder at an angle of somewhat more than ninety degrees. The sheet is large, is not stretched, its percale accommodates her motion. She is a large woman. She was a big young girl. She had a mixture of depth of sensuality and of innocence that intrigued him, almost irresistibly, even when he was afraid he might be doing something wrong. But all they did together, the most intimate thing, was to run off under the low, overhanging branches of some trees and kiss. The sheet, as she turns now to the right, makes the sound of the leaves of those trees.

THE MOOR OF VENICE

Othello was a Black American painter living in Venice. He had a studio in the Dòrsoduro and very often in the daytime he sat in his favorite café on the Giudecca, looking at everything and everybody, talking, and drinking wine. His Desdemona was an aristocratic girl. She was not very pretty but she was very Venetian, which is not precisely the same as being very Italian. She lived with her family in a gigantic and pleasing palace, near (two palaces away) the one in which Byron had lived. If you rode down the Grand Canal, you could see the chandeliers glittering through windows into the night.

The Duca Di Duro liked Othello's paintings, and bought some. That is how the painter met Isabella Di Duro. She was his *belle laide* and he her *mécontent*. Her father, a gentle and rather effeminate man, was sleepily troubled and wryly twisted by this relationship. Isabella's mother, the duchess, was scandalized, but knew the love affair would end. Tolavon painted a large yellow and orange portrait of Isabella.

Her father bought the painting. It was not only for his black skin that Tolavon was called Othello. He was also violently jealous. After three months of knowing Isabella, he came one afternoon to the Palazzo Duro, and saw her with her arms around another man's neck and her body against his. The white handkerchief pinched in her fingers looked like a rose; the stem was Augusto Del Tavo's spine. Othello walked past them, took a knife, and slashed at his canvas. He could as easily have slashed them. Instead he walked past violently to the door.

The man was Isabella's cousin, just back from his travels in the United States. Seeing the Tolavon canvas, he cried, Ah a Tolavon, a great one, the best I've ever seen! Isabella, moved by his enthusiasm, had thrown her arms around his neck. Isabella bravely went after Tolavon and found him—after three days. At first he wouldn't believe her. Then he did. Afterward, he was milder.

He repainted the painting. It was better in some ways and less good in others than the first one, and on the whole it was quite a different work. The duke liked it less but took it and hung it in his palazzo. It pleased him and troubled him; he was worried about his daughter. The sunlight blazed into the palazzo windows. His ancestor Andrea Di Duro had been right to construct a palace on the afternoon-sun side of the canal. Tolavon was pleased to have his big painting hanging there. He even thought of changing his café, since from the one where he now sat, facing the Giudecca, the duke's palace couldn't be seen. He didn't do that, however. He did put some lire down and stood up and left his table and walked. Tolavon was beginning to be known and to sell his work. An independent life, and freedom, unrolled like flat waves at his feet.

Now, though, he stood out in the Dòrsoduro air, waiting for Isabella to come along. He felt the sea in the canal air on his skin. Putting a finger to his cheek, he found it came away cool, and damp—condensation!

Keep up your bright swords, for the dew will rust them, Shakespeare's Othello said. This one, Tolavon-Othello, had an idea for a painting: Isabella standing, with the dew-wet, misty Palladio, San Giorgio Maggiore, on the island just across from him, at her back.

THE WISH TO BE PREGNANT

A bird just sat on a tree branch outside my living room window and when it opened its beak, bubbles came out. They looked like soap bubbles. I have no idea what they actually were.

Serenity was not a main subject or even concern of the New York painters. A big bully of a guy, named Haggis Coptics, was strutting around the bars.

It was spring, and the alloys in the earth were melting. I saw my wife with the pot in which a chestnut soup was cooking. Right after our marriage she began to cook exotic and flavorsome foods. I half-expected quickly to grow fat in this marriage, as L. Tagenquist had in his, but I did not. It was only a few years after this that mildly excessive eating began to cause me to put on some weight. One morning I looked in the mirror—"You are much too fat!"

A valentine was exchanged for a handclasp then a kiss and then finally another valentine from the shop. Held hands veered downstreet together. For one the holiday had not replaced feeling at all. But this one was a dog.

Hello, said Jerry, coming up from behind me with a blindfold in his hand that, he said, he had just tied around the eyes of a girl. I fucked her in the basement, he said. Well, that's better than doing nothing, huh?

My wife came in from the kitchen. Lunch is ready, she said. Then, Oh, how I want to have a child!